# RUN
## with the
# MOON

## DIANA DERICCI

Purple Sword Publications
Tucson, AZ

**RUN WITH THE MOON**
Copyright © 2015 DIANA DERICCI
ISBN 978-1-61292-140-2
ISBN 10: 161292140X
Cover Art Designed by Anastasia Rabiyah
Image Copyright Dan Skinner
Edited by Traci Markou

Published by Purple Sword Publications, LLC
Tucson, Arizona, USA
www.PurpleSword.com

## Chapter One

Howls ricocheted through the woods like the haunting sound of a pending storm, like a surreal thunder. The eerie brush and scratch of trees and leaves was unsettling because nothing moved. There was no wind, no other sounds.

Except for those howls.

They echoed around Jamie on all sides. He knew he was surrounded. He could only pray that the pack didn't close in. He was fucked if they did. Wasn't much he could do with a single backpack against a pack of wolves. He didn't even have a knife.

Jamie huddled beneath the thickest bower of limbs, his stomach rumbling. He ignored it. He had to ration what he had managed to stuff in his bag.

He closed his eyes and drew a steadying breath, refusing to let the shakes overtake him again. Five days wasn't that long. He'd be in a new town or city soon, and he could start over. Find a job. Find a place to live, even if it was only a dry corner somewhere.

His eyes burst open when the next round of howls started. Sharper, closer. He shivered. Jamie knew the animals were taunting him, trying to flush him out. The fastest way to agitate a predator was to run. Cowards ran.

His head sank to his huddled knees, swamped in on all sides by his melancholy and situation. He guessed then that he was a coward. He'd run from his father's fist. So much to ignore. His empty stomach. The burning pull on his ribs. The aching stiffness of his jaw. The gnawing pain and ache in his arm. *Those relentless howls.* Gingerly he touched his lip; it felt like the swelling had gone down, but he couldn't say. He hadn't seen his face at its worst or since he'd run from the house after his father's last drunken rage.

The night was a refuge of sorts. It was quiet, and not too cold. Tucked into his body there was a modicum of warmth, but not much. It took him a few minutes to realize the howls had ceased. He lifted his chin, searching with unblinking eyes into the dark shadows around him. The highway was silent at that time of night, somewhere off to his right. He'd dug into the trees for cover and shelter in case the weather turned bad. It had the night before. He only had a couple changes of clothes with him. There had been pain in every motion as he'd stuffed his old backpack with clothes, energy bars, and two bottles of water as quickly as possible. He only had the one pair of sneakers.

Jamie sniffled, wincing for it. He was twenty-two, and until five nights ago had never thought his father would be able to kill him. He'd been hit. Plenty. He knew without a doubt now that his father hated him. Jamie had mistakenly believed his dad had needed him. He'd stayed after graduation to help his dad. Help pay bills. It wasn't like either of them had ever had much.

Telling him Jamie was gay had been the straw that broke the camel's back.

The last thing he remembered after the ominous silence of his admission was disappearing into his bedroom and getting ready for bed. He had work the next morning. Three hours later, he'd been bodily yanked out of bed and attacked. Jamie had never seen his dad that drunk in his life. Jamie had fought back, instinctively knowing that this time if he didn't, his dad would kill him. With all the strength he had, he'd swung one of his long-ago track trophies at his father's head. He was so drunk he hadn't gone down instantly, staggering and teetering instead like a chopped tree, defying before finally giving in to gravity. Jamie had leaped across his bed, putting it between them, watching. Then, almost as if his dad's body just hit a switch, he'd collapsed across Jamie's bed.

Blood seeped from a cut on the back of his head by his ear, but that was all the damage he'd done. Snores that should have woken the dead were echoed by heavy breathing. He was out.

Jamie had stuffed what he could into his backpack and left. He had no job now and only minimal cash on hand. He prayed when he finally found a place to stop, he could call and get his last paycheck, but he wasn't holding his breath for life to treat him right. After twenty-two years, he should know better.

Five nights after that fight, he was somewhere west of home, heading somewhere far away from a life that had been nothing but pain-filled and disappointing.

He blinked into the shadows as another chorus began.

*And I'm surrounded by wolves.* "Yay," he croaked. He flipped the hood up on his sweatshirt, burrowing his hands into the pockets. As snug as he could be, he clung tighter to his bent legs and closed his eyes, listening, but trying to rest before he started walking again.

* * * *

Weak sunlight woke Jamie from the doze he'd finally managed. Joints creaked and protested profusely when he shifted and stretched. Gamely, he used flat palms to brace himself on the tree behind him to force himself to his feet. Retrieving his pack, he unzipped it and dug out a bottle of water, sucking a few hard swallows before recapping it and putting it in with his clothes again. It was all he had until he found a way to replenish or a place to stop.

He was in the middle of nowhere, between Bumfuck and somewhere over the rainbow, so for now he was still moving. Pushing low-lying limbs out of his path, he found the highway again and started walking. He didn't put out a thumb. Jamie wasn't crazy enough to hitch along with everything else. With the way he looked, beaten three ways to Sunday and more rumpled than a wadded sheet of paper, no one would pick him up anyway. Jamie was fine with that. He wouldn't be able to explain his condition without the fear that the next person he told would want to repeat it—or worse. There were plenty of hate crimes and murders in the news that were related to sexuality.

Grimacing, he just wasn't going to do that. With a plodded determination he began walking, putting more distance between himself and his past. The sun had moved quite a bit before he dug in his bag for one of the few bars he'd dumped in there. He tried not to wolf it down, but they weren't meant to be a sole meal and it only took a couple bites and another swig of water to wash it down before it was gone. He stuffed the trash into a side pocket and kept walking.

A couple cars passed him in the opposite direction. He didn't pay them any attention. They were going the wrong way to begin with, and none of them even slowed as they roared by.

Jamie didn't know the time, other than it had to be close to noon by the sun beating down on him, when a pickup slowed at his side.

The tinted window came down. "Hey, kid."

Jamie looked up cautiously, getting a view of the inside and the driver.

"Need a ride?"

He shook his head.

The driver gave him a once-over. There was genuine concern in his pale gray eyes. Jamie was sure he looked like the walking dead.

"Are you sure? Silo's still another three miles, at least."

"I'm fine." He barely managed it, his voice raw and dry.

The driver took another speculative look. "When did you eat last?"

Jamie's heart tripped. *Food?* He swallowed slowly. There wasn't any way to stifle the growl of his stomach at just the thought of something more solid than a granola bar two or three hours ago. He didn't doubt in the least that the other guy heard it, though he showed no sign of it.

The driver leaned across the cloth seat and popped open the door. "I'm not going to hurt you," he said soothingly. "I'm going to my brother's for lunch. Come eat. It'll at least get you into town."

Jamie studied him. Of the cars that had driven by that day, so far this was the only one to even slow, much less offer a ride. Jamie was fine with that, except... *Food.* Yeah, that was more than he could fight.

The guy behind the wheel had camel-brown hair, cut short and trimmed, a broad chest as well as wide hands on the steering wheel, and those miss-nothing gray eyes. He knew it was in his best interest to refuse again, but the offer of food... His stomach cramped this time.

"I can't pay you," he finally managed, his voice graveled.

The driver offered a slight smile. "Wasn't expecting you to. Come on. Cade makes a mean burger." He physically tipped toward the driver's door, rather than threatening Jamie's space.

Jamie couldn't keep himself from licking his lips with that news. Real food. Something hot and filling. *Oh God.* He couldn't ignore the hunger slicing his stomach into shreds at the opportunity for something substantial. Giving in, he grudgingly placed his pack on the floorboards and aware of his own state of disaster, he tugged off his hoodie and turned it inside-out to sit on. "Sorry for the mess."

He got a shrugged shoulder in answer. "Buckle up. I like to jump the ravine on the way."

Jamie shot him a wide-eyed, heart-stopping stare.

A guffawing laugh filled the truck cab. "Playing, man. Just playing." He put on his blinker to get on the road. "I'm Chris."

Jamie tucked his arms around his middle and tried to hug the door. "Jamie."

"Nice to meet you." Chris slid him a quick glance before retraining his vision on the road. "You been walking a while?"

"A few days."

Chris grunted, but didn't add to it or ask more. A few minutes later, the bell of a cell phone rang. He tugged it from a pocket. "Yep." Jamie couldn't help but listen in the confines of the truck cab. "I'm on my way. Don't you dare burn mine for being late. Brat. I told you the Mathison's mare was going to foal this morning, and she did. At four in the damned morning." Jamie heard his laugh, a slow husky sound that made the hair on his forearms stand up. "Yeah, well, toss on a couple more. I'm bringing a friend. Okay, be there soon."

"A mare?" Jamie asked after he'd ended the call.

Chris hooked a thumb toward the bed of the truck. "Traveling veterinarian."

Jamie peered over a shoulder, actually seeing the bins and equipment for the first time. He hadn't thought anything of it at all when Chris had first stopped at Jamie's feet on the roadside.

"My brothers and I own the town's clinic, and I drew the short straw this week."

"I'm sorry?"

"We trade weeks to do the emergency overnight on-calls. This is my week."

"Oh," he murmured, curling against the door again. He didn't try to make more small talk, and thankfully Chris didn't seem to want any or interested in asking questions to fill the quiet.

A few minutes later, he began to see signs of the town. "Silo?" Jamie asked.

"All nine thousand of us."

"Wow."

"A lot of close-knit families, small businesses, schools, and base structures. We're a pretty self-sufficient little burg."

Too small to get lost in, in other words. That was okay for Jamie. He'd keep going until he found a larger city, somewhere even his dad wouldn't be able to find him, if he were bothered to try. Where Jamie would just be another nameless person in a faceless crowd. No one would know who he was. Maybe he'd just keep going until he hit something big, like mountains or the ocean. He'd always heard the West Coast was nice. Maybe he'd keep going until he got there.

Lost in tumultuous thoughts, it took the call of his name to pull him out of the darkness.

"Jamie?"

He straightened, focusing blankly on the man in the truck.

"We're here."

Jamie looked the other direction out the window and spotted the small, squat house, which was a faint blue color. Chris had parked at the curb. There was another pickup in the driveway.

Jamie scrambled from the truck, flipping his hoodie to put it on and hook his backpack over a shoulder. "You're sure he won't mind an extra mouth to feed?" Jamie hesitated by the truck. Chris waited patiently on the sidewalk. Jamie's nerves were kicking in harder now that he was there. He didn't know Chris or his brother Cade. He could forego another meal. He'd barely eaten in almost five days. Another two or three wouldn't kill him. He looked down the street one way, then the other, and wondered how far the next town was.

"Cade always makes too much anyway," Chris told him. He hooked a thumb into his front jeans pocket. Jamie watched him take a deep sniff. "Smells good."

Jamie couldn't help but do the same, and his mouth watered. Hard. He swallowed. His stomach growled so loud, he put an arm around his middle. An arched eyebrow from Chris proved he wouldn't be able to hide it this time or act like he wasn't starving.

## Chapter Two

Chris waited on the sidewalk without moving a muscle. He would have waited all day for Jamie to decide. Turned out the next wave of grilled beef on the breeze did the trick. He shuffled up to Chris's side, though not close, his head down. At least he hadn't covered his head again. Without saying anything more, Chris led him to the backyard.

"Hey! About time," Cade called when he caught Chris's gaze as they rounded the house. Chris flashed him a look, twitching with a miniscule effort of his chin behind him. Cade's eyes widened in surprise, then he smiled, a known attempt to soften the gruffness of his features.

Chris heard Jamie's steps falter when he cleared the corner of the house.

Chris made the introductions. "Cade, Jamie."

"Hi, Jamie." Cade glanced at Chris, who shook his head once. Cade didn't offer a hand.

"Hi." Jamie all but whispered it. He clutched his backpack strap like a lifeline.

Cade waved toward Jamie's shoulder. "You can put that on the table over there. There's tea all ready. Help yourselves."

Chris usually helped Cade with the cooking but in this instance, he walked over to the table and poured two glasses instead. Warily, Jamie followed him. He guessed compared to Cade, he was the

10

lesser of two evils. Cade was a big guy compared to Chris's compact size. Cade was six-three where Chris was five-eleven. Cade also looked like a tattooed biker on a good day, with his wild auburn hair to his shoulders. Cade was definitely the wilder one of the brothers.

He offered the iced tea. "Here." He waited until Jamie raised his eyes before trying to hand him the glass. "Drink it slowly. You're probably dehydrated, and it'll make you cramp if you gulp it."

Jamie frowned. "I'm not—"

"Not a people doctor, but I know enough. Okay?" he said gently.

Jamie's pinched lips only exacerbated the abuse they were healing from. Lashes lowered to hide enigmatic blue eyes that were so deeply shadowed with sleep deprivation they looked smudged. Whatever had happened it had been bad, with all the bruising and fading swelling. And that was only what Chris could see. He sincerely doubted it was limited to his face. He hadn't had a chance to see in the truck and Jamie had put the hoodie back on, covering his skin. With a flash of insight, he realized Jamie was wearing a long-sleeved shirt beneath it. The reasoning behind that in the May heat made his stomach curdle. Thick bronze-blond hair that curled around his ears was the only other feature Chris could be sure of.

He also knew, had known the instant he'd opened his window, that this was the same person he and his pack had discovered in the woods last night. Not because he was dirty, or male, or alone. But because even then, as bad as he looked, as woeful, hurting and as lost as he seemed, Chris wanted to curl around him and keep him safe. His wolf had known last night but he hadn't been able to do anything about it except tell his pack what he'd found, what they'd almost stumbled on last night and likely would have terrified right into hysteria.

After their run last night, his plan had been to return to the woods and find him. Figure out what the story was behind why he was hiding in the woods and help him. Except the Mathison's mare had pulled his priorities in another direction. He was going to ask Cade to help him track tonight to find this young man again.

Unexpectedly, Chris had found him trudging along the side of the westbound two-lane highway moving toward town instead. He watched Jamie carefully from the corner of his eye so he wouldn't feel like a spectacle. He was pale, thin, and in need of some major TLC and nourishment. And a very light touch. He wasn't a big guy like either Chris or Cade, maybe five-seven and light of build, like a reed. He had long fingers and narrow hips. The fact that he'd been someone's punching bag was merely an inarguable observation.

Jamie took his advice and drank slowly, taking a couple minutes to down half the glass.

"This is good," Jamie said, tapping the plastic with a finger. He took another couple swallows and looked at the pitcher.

"Help yourself," Chris told him. "I'm going to see if Cade needs anything. All right?"

Jamie nodded, finally unhooking his pack and laying it on the ground by the picnic table leg.

That helped Chris to relax, seeing Jamie become comfortable as well. He placed his own glass of tea on the table and then walked over to the grill and his brother. "The rest inside?"

"On the counter."

"I'll grab it." With a nod of thanks from Cade, Chris went through the rear screen door heading for the kitchen. He found a covered platter filled with stuff to stick on a burger like lettuce and tomatoes, plus cheese and bacon strips as well as ketchup and mustard. Cade must have realized something was up when Chris told him he was bringing a friend. He *never* bothered with vegetables. They weren't on his palatable list. With his hands full of plates, the platter, and bottles he nudged the screen door open with a toe and a hip, then wove to the table.

Jamie was still standing and immediately leaped to help Chris, taking the plates off the top.

"Thanks," Chris said.

"Welcome."

"Did you grab the chips?" Cade called from his position in front of the grill.

"No. Pantry?"

"Yeah."

"Do you need more help?" Jamie asked, almost too quietly to hear.

Chris gazed at him, sorry when Jamie didn't lift his own eyes. "No. Just a couple bags of chips to go with everything."

Jamie moved a shoulder. "Okay."

"Thanks, though."

"S-sure," he replied unsteadily.

Chris repeated his trip, carrying two bags of chips to the table just as Cade slid a stacked tower of meat onto the table. "Lunch is served, gentlemen."

Chris saw Jamie gulp, his eyes on the stack. Shock or hunger? Hunger, yes, but *definitely* shock. The brothers could put four away each, no problem, twice that if it was the full moon cycle.

It seemed Jamie was trying for some restraint with the speed he devoured his burger, either because he wasn't alone or maybe from Chris's caution of earlier. Chris topped off his tea with hardly a slowdown of his own eating.

"How is the foal?" Cade asked more than a burger and a half later.

"Cute as a button. Filly this time."

"Mr. M's happy, huh?"

"He wanted another Dandy so bad," Chris replied with a smile, remembering that morning's chaos and the resulting birth. The filly was the spitting image of her dam. Chris sat beside Cade, giving Jamie the whole other side of the table. He didn't want the younger man to feel threatened by the brothers.

"So, where are you headed, Jamie?"

Chris immediately knocked their knees together with a dull thwack. Jamie stopped chewing, his hands holding the burger trembling in the wake of the question. Tension filled the silence around the table now. Chris gave Cade a dirty look.

*Sorry,* he mouthed silently.

"West, I think," Jamie finally muttered, though he didn't look up, blatantly avoiding their stares.

"Eat what you want," Chris said kindly, redirecting Jamie's focus off himself, still using the tone he did with a frightened animal because there was no doubt Jamie was terrified. It took a few minutes, but Jamie started eating again. He never did look up. That, more than anything, tugged at Chris.

He couldn't begin to guess what the other man had been through, but he had a good idea. The marks all over him told a story. It wasn't pretty, and it didn't have a happy ending.

In the end, Jamie ate two burgers and countless handfuls of chips before saying he was full. His eyelids drooped where he sat with sunlight beating down on them in the early afternoon. Gradually snaps of wind had been picking up, signaling a change in the weather.

Chris helped Cade clean up. Jamie tried to help, stacking things at the table, but he didn't try to follow them into the house. Chris was almost scared he'd be gone, already trying to move on before he could come back outside.

"What are you going to do?" Cade asked over his shoulder with Chris right behind him once they were inside.

"I don't know. Should I take him home?"

"Good luck getting him to agree. That kid's been through hell."

Chris dumped stuff in the trash, then moved to the sink to wash his hands. "Maybe a night to clean up and rest. Think he'd want to do that?" Chris couldn't let him go. He'd figure out a way to convince him to stay for longer. He had to. Just had to have a chance. He dried his hands as he waited for Cade's opinion.

Cade looked out the window in the kitchen. "Hey. Think that might help your argument?"

Chris came to stand at his shoulder and gazed into the distance with him. A thick band of ominous black was rolling in, the cause behind the surges of wind. "I don't think I've ever been thankful for a squall line, but I'll take it."

"Quade isn't going to let you off your on-call because you took in a stray."

"I know. Hopefully, it'll stay quiet."

Cade gave him an arched eyebrow. The odds…yeah, not all that good. He'd have to take the chance.

"You're sure he's the one from last night?"

"Positive," Chris answered. "I'm just glad I didn't lose him after we were done running."

Cade tilted his head. "I think he's about to bolt."

Chris heard it too: the sound of movement, Jamie's backpack. "I'll talk to you later," he called as he bounded for the back door, catching the handle to brace himself before he threw himself through the doorway and likely scare Jamie into next week.

Cade was right. Jamie was standing near the table when he opened it, focused on the north skies. He'd seen the storm line too.

"I need to get going. Thank you for the burgers." He dug a hand into his worn jeans. The strap of his backpack was centered on his shoulder already.

"Do you have a place to go?" Chris asked gently.

Jamie glanced away. "I…" He took in the line of thunderstorms bearing down on them. His shoulders caved. "No."

Chris could tell by the way he kept looking to the north, he really didn't want to be out when those storms swept through.

"Why don't you come to my house? You can take a shower, get some decent rest."

Jamie looked at him through his lashes suspiciously. "I can't pay you."

"Don't want your money, even if you have any," Chris reiterated. When Jamie still hesitated, Chris said, "I know you're running from something. Let me help you."

"I'm not a kid." Jamie growled.

"I guessed you were at least eighteen."

"I'm twenty-two," he snapped under his breath, half-turned away. A deep inhale rocked Jamie's shoulders. "You're not going to chop me up and bury me in the basement, are you?"

"I don't have a basement. I might have room in the barn," Chris replied with droll seriousness.

Jamie hopped a step away.

"Riiiiiight." Chris rolled his eyes. "Not out to hurt you, Jamie."

The ominous rumble of thunder a few seconds later drew both their attentions toward the impending line of storms.

"Give yourself a break, Jamie. One night. I'll even drive you out of town tomorrow to make sure you get a safe start."

Chris pushed his tongue against his teeth to not make more promises. He had plenty he could make.

Another hot meal, or three. Clean clothes. Safety. A soft bed. Protection. Fresh water.

But he forced himself to lean on a hip like he had all the time in the world. Honestly, he just wanted to go home and relax. He'd been up and going since four that morning with the new foal. He'd been home briefly to shower and change, then Cade had urged him to come to lunch and Chris wasn't going to turn down food. He was on-call but unless it was dire, everyone knew to go to the clinic if they could. They had the best equipment there and more supplies.

Seconds before Chris was about to offer anything and probably screw it all up, Jamie faced him. There was a firm scowl in place.

"One night."

"One night," Chris agreed. It was a start. It was all he needed.

## Chapter Three

Jamie knew he was insane. He was going home with a complete and utter stranger. Granted, he'd been nice enough to feed Jamie, but he knew nothing else about Chris. He was a vet of some sort. Jamie knew even less about what they did, other than they fixed broken animals. Silo seemed to be a very small town, and Cade's house was one of about half a dozen on that particular street.

He tried to take a more interested snapshot of Silo as they left, but was sadly disappointed. There were roughly two blocks of local stores, with a post office at the end at a blinking yellow light. Back the way they had come in was a small grocery store and the almost obligatory railroad tracks across the main two-lane road.

Jamie took in the signs and sat up a little straighter as he got a mental map going of the town. "Is that a library?" The brick exterior looked to be newer and very well cared-for compared to some of the other buildings on the main street, which showed considerably marked age on their facades.

"It is. It's not big, but they work with the surrounding counties for book exchanges and even have Internet for those who can't get it at home."

"Is it that expensive out here?"

"Not really. Some of the homes are very rural. The center of Silo only has a few hundred living here. Cade's house? One of the original town settlers. He didn't have any family, and Cade put a bid on it through the city. No one expected him to get it, but he's happy. Quade has a small cabin by the clinic, and I'm in our original home."

"Three of you?"

Chris nodded. "Cade and Quade are twins."

"You're kidding!" Jamie couldn't fathom that. Cade was *huge.*

Chris chuckled with a throaty depth. "And I'm the oldest."

Jamie slid him a sideways glance. "How old?"

"Ancient," Chris mused. "Twenty-nine."

Jamie ran a finger over the outer seam of his jeans along his thigh. They were all so young. And yet, they seemed happy. A contented place in at least Chris and Cade's life that Jamie wasn't sure he'd ever felt. "Parents?"

Chris's focus fell from the road to the dash. "They died four years ago."

Jamie gasped, the answer unexpected. "I'm sorry," he said.

"Dad was the town vet, and I was already working for him. We'd all been raised around it so going into veterinary medicine wasn't a hard choice, though the boys had the option to do something else if they wanted. I made sure Cade and Quade could afford to go for whatever they wanted. We hold it together. So long as nobody throws something like an elephant or an exotic at us, we're capable. There's also a larger hospital in Stiller Springs. We can recommend them on a moment's notice, and they'll take our patients."

"That's good support. Is that why you drive to them? Because there's so many?"

"It's easier on them, usually. A foaling mare or a herniated cow are no fun to transport."

"No, I imagine not."

"It's pretty routine usually."

Conversation fell off again, only this time it was a serene calm. A lot easier on Jamie's nerves. He noticed that once they were out of town, Chris turned right onto another road. Farms or solitary homes were placed well off in the distance.

"Definitely out in the country," Jamie muttered. Not a soul in sight.

"That's not necessarily a bad thing," Chris offered.

*It is if you don't want to be found.* Jamie just wrapped his arms around his middle and gazed out the window. He wasn't all that sure his dad would try to look for him. He just didn't want to make it easy if he did.

The bump of changing from road to dirt brought Jamie to his present situation. Fenced pasture ran on both sides of the narrow drive, with the house at the end on the edge of a circle drive.

The outside was faded wood and rugged, a ranch-style home with a nice covered porch that went corner to corner along the front. It all looked homey and welcoming. Chris drove past the house and slowed in front of a barn.

"I need to dump a few things in the waste bin. Give me a minute." Chris hopped out of the truck and wound to the back, letting down the gate.

Jamie cautiously got out, standing by his door. The air was growing heavier with the pending rain and sharp winds beginning to snap around them, the precursor to the storms. He watched Chris dig out a plastic trash bag from somewhere in the truck. It didn't look like Chris needed any help so he stayed out of the way, hanging on the open door with his uninjured arm.

A pounding racket pulled his attention to the side of the barn. A large, black horse with white socks charged the fence, neighing. He tossed his head, waving a glossy black mane that hung well past his neck.

"Wow," Jamie choked out.

Chris made some clucking noises in their direction that seemed to get a whicker in answer. "That's Tiberius. His shadow is Biscuit."

Moving around the door Jamie could see the smaller horse, a pony noticeably smaller in size. "He's actually kind of cute."

"He was a rescue. Some dumb cluck bought him for his kid thinking his son could just hop on him like the Lone Ranger and all would be right in the world. A lot of people don't realize that even a horse that size weighs several hundred pounds against a kid who weighs less than eighty."

"Doesn't sound like it ended well for the boy," Jamie said, sliding his gaze to Chris, listening as he finished at the truck and closed it up. He paused near Jamie before carrying everything to the barn door.

"It didn't. Biscuit threw him like a sack of potatoes, and the kid broke a leg. I found out after I had him and examined him that the boy had whipped him like a piñata. Now he won't let anyone small near him. Can't blame him. I've been working with him, but he's got issues. Ponies are also well known for being the assholes of the equine world. Once they're there, they don't usually come back from the dark side."

"That's a shame." Jamie tilted his head to study the little yellow beast. One of the large sliding doors opened on the barn a moment later. He waited for Chris to return before continuing. "What's Tiberius's story?"

Chris came and stood at the truck fender. "He's my wagon horse. I hitch him up a couple times a year and do wagon rides for the kids. Usually for the Fall Festival around Halloween and for Christmas."

A fresh gust of wind reminded them of the incoming weather. Chris looked over his shoulder to study the sky.

"Let me get these two inside, then we'll be set."

"Okay."

Chris opened a gate nearby and walked up to the monster horse. He towered over Chris when he curled a hand through the strap on Tiberius's head. "Inside, boy." The big black head shook, then Tiberius followed obediently, Biscuit on his heels.

A few minutes later Chris reappeared, closing the barn door and snapping the fence gate shut.

"We better get inside. This is fixing to break loose any minute," Chris called, clambering up into the truck.

\* \* \* \*

Chris stood at the window in the living room watching the roiling storm march in on them.

Lightning illuminated the tops of the billowed clouds. Not ten minutes after they walked in, the skies opened up. It was almost as dark as nighttime outside now.

Chris had shown Jamie the spare room a few minutes ago, and it had been silent since then. He replayed those moments through his mind, trying to find the key to Jamie's trust.

"You're sure?"

"Jamie." Chris sighed with a hint of exasperation. He had no idea what Jamie was expecting, but Chris was *not* going to chop him up.

"Okay," Jamie relented. He dropped the pack at his feet just inside the door. "Is that the bathroom?" He pointed across the room.

"Closet. Bathroom is one door down." Chris leaned out of the doorway where he'd stopped. "Help yourself." He started to turn away, then said, "Oh, I have some laundry to do if you want to toss in your things."

He really didn't, but he'd find something. Jamie's were a mess.

"I don't have anything clean to change into," Jamie said in a very quiet voice. His gaze fell to the floor.

"It's okay," Chris offered with a soothing lightness. "There's plenty here. Look in the closet or in the dresser. This was Cade's old room. I'm sure there's something."

Chris went to step away to give him space.

"Chris?"

"Yes?"

"Thank you."

"You're welcome. Come out when you're ready."

Staring out into the raging storm, Chris was still waiting.

Eventually he heard doors open and then water running through the house. It raised a small, hopeful smile. He took the phone out of his pocket and dialed the clinic.

"Dr. Rose Animal Clinic."

"Hi, Lyla. Is Quade busy?"

"Nope. Just finished a checkup. The storm chased everyone else out. Hold on."

He shifted his weight to a hip. Lightning flashed with a crack of thunder that sounded directly overhead. Good thing he came home when he did. He wouldn't have wanted the horses out in this.

"Dr. Rose."

"It's me."

"How'd the foaling go?"

Chris studied the falling rain. "Smooth as could be."

"Good."

"I found him," Chris said a little quieter. "He's been beaten bad, though."

"Damn." Quade sighed. "Is he okay?"

"Skittish." Chris turned with half his focus to the rest of the house to listen for Jamie. "I'm going to try to convince him to stay. I don't know how to do this, Quade." He rubbed the back of his neck. "I wish Mom and Dad were still here."

"You could talk to Alpha about it," Quade suggested. "It's been a while since anyone had an outsider for a mate. He might have some advice."

Chris noticed when the shower turned off. "I'll think about it." Chris's eyes shot upward when the lights flickered under another crashing boom, then winked out. "Crap."

"Power." Quade grumbled. "Let me start the generator. I hope this doesn't last too long. I'll talk to you later."

Then the phone went quiet.

"Um, Chris?"

"Yeah?" He faced Jamie, standing before him in a towel and nothing else. His mouth went dry.

Droplets clung to the ends of his hair, and the scent of warm skin and soap filled Chris's nose. He shook himself. He'd been right. Jamie was in need of several meals, waif-thin, and black and blue in spots too large to hide. Many, too many really, were fresh, while others were obviously old and healing, in varying shades of yellow. He'd known, but seeing it, seeing how much he'd been hurt, how much he was *still* hurting, killed Chris.

"Jamie," he whispered. He went to take a step closer, and stopped after one. "Who did that?"

Jamie looked down, as though unaware of what the issue was. Chris was able to see, even in the murky darkness of the blocked sun, when Jamie's face paled. Jamie slid a protective arm over his middle, for all the little it could hide; the rest remained exposed.

"It's nothing."

Chris took another tentative step. Jamie twitched with the energy to escape. "Someone did, Jamie. Is that why you ran?"

Jamie looked away, his throat working hard. Tension filled his features. "I...I wanted...to make sure..." he stammered.

"Anything, Jamie," Chris said, now only an arm's length away.

Jamie scrunched his eyes and exhaled sharply, his head twisted to look to the side. His eyes glowed boldly when he turned them full force on Chris. "Why are you being so nice? What do you want from me?"

"Because it's who I am, and I don't want anything from you."

Jamie huffed in disbelief. "There's something. There always is." He cleared his throat. "I wanted to make sure about the clothes," he said firmly, devoid of the emotions that were so clearly plaguing him.

"Sure, Jamie. If it fits, go for it."

"Thank you."

Before Chris could reply, Jamie slipped off into the hallway and through the bedroom door, as gone as a ghost in the dark.

# Chapter Four

Jamie sat on the bed with a clean shirt clutched in his hand. The lights were still out, and except for that momentary panic when they'd died just as he was getting out of the shower, he was okay with that. Less he'd have to explain if Chris couldn't see him clearly. He couldn't see very well in the room because of the outage, so he was doing several things by feel. He'd lucked into a worn pair of jeans in the closet that were too loose and bunched around his ankles, but he could adjust most of that. He was pretty sure they were older, meaning too small for Cade, which was why they were still there to begin with. Cade was twice Jamie's size, easy.

The shirt he held was just an old T-shirt with something ironed on the front, a design he couldn't quite make out in the darkness. After meeting Cade, he'd be willing to bet it was something bordering on vulgar. He could see that in a younger Cade.

He let out a slow breath. Chris, on the other hand… Jamie *wished* he could figure him out, even a little.

He was still at a loss over why he was being so helpful to begin with. Granted, Jamie hadn't left home a full week before, yet even before then, so few were able to look him in the eye at work. He knew several suspected the reasons he always wore long-sleeved shirts, even in the summer. Exposure of any part wasn't an option. And none had so much as given a single hand to help him.

Chris was giving him a hand, a roof, food. Looking at the door, Jamie was positive there was a reason. And he feared what it could be. Even worse, the repercussions if Chris learned he was gay. How would he feel about helping a *gay* man? A fresh shiver struck, and it wasn't because he was damp in spots.

The driving need to be covered was part of why he was still sitting on the bed holding the T-shirt instead of dressing in it. He ran a light cupped hand down his left forearm. The swelling lingered. He was positive one of the bones was cracked. He'd deflected a crushing blow to his head with it, and it still hurt like hell. The swelling had been bad the first three nights, but keeping it covered had kept Chris from asking any questions. Jamie didn't want to answer them. He hadn't found any long-sleeved shirts in the mishmash of the closet or dresser.

The T-shirt was one of a few, and the only option. All of his things were rank and desperate for a wash. He didn't have that much, and he could only change things so many times in five days.

A wave of thunder rolled, signaling the passing of the storm, and almost like a snap of fingers the lights came back on.

The freedom of darkness was gone. Staring blankly at his arm, he couldn't do anything about that, but he pulled on the T-shirt regardless. He bent to grab the hoodie off his backpack to slide it on over everything just as there was a tap on the door.

"Jamie?"

The call of his name had him rush to cover up. "Yeah?" He didn't move off the bed. The bedroom door opened.

"Now that the power's on, I'm going to do those clothes. What have you got?"

Gray eyes swept over him, clearly noticing he was in his hoodie again. "Let me bring it. It's pretty nasty."

Chris flashed a grin. "Have you any idea *what* I get covered in?"

Jamie blinked. "Uh, no, I guess not." He wasn't sure he wanted to know, either.

Chris held out a hand. Accepting the inevitable in this case, he gathered the small bundle, including his stash from his backpack, and gave Chris the wad.

"What about that?" Chris asked, giving a meaning-filled look to the black sweatshirt hiding him.

"I'll keep it."

"Okay." Then he walked away.

*He didn't push?* Jamie didn't know what to think. Barefoot, Jamie trailed Chris, getting a better look at the house. It was compact like Cade's, but open with the bedrooms and spare bath on one half and the kitchen and living room on the other half. The washer and dryer were in a small room off the kitchen.

The trill of the cell phone came from Chris's pocket. He answered as he filled the washer and added soap. "Hello. Hey, yeah, we're fine. Power just came back on a few minutes ago. How is it there? Good. If you need me let me know, but I'm going to relax for a few hours. Hopefully it's quiet tonight. Okay. Later." He disconnected and absently slid it back into a pocket.

"Everything okay?" Jamie asked, hoping he wasn't intruding.

"Yeah. Just Quade checking in. Their electricity just came back on too. They're all okay. It can get rough out there depending on what the storms whip up."

"All three of you are vets?"

Chris nodded. "Quade has the most education, I have the most equine experience, and Cade has the most brains."

"Really?"

Chris chuckled, closing the washer lid. "I know. You'd never expect it from him with the tattoos. We have a few employees, an accountant, and all the important stuff." Chris faced him, leaning with a hip on the gurgling machine. After a thoughtful once-over, he said, "Ever thought of working with animals? I bet you'd be good. You're very calm."

"Me?" Jamie squeaked. He backed up when Chris straightened. He'd been working for a local grocery store since before he graduated. There wasn't any sign of college in his future. He knew his options were nil with his dad anyway.

"Yeah, sure. Why not?"

Jamie shrugged, then crossed his arms. What could he say? *I couldn't go to school because my dad is an alcoholic and I was the one covering the bills*? His dad had needed him, but not the way Jamie had wanted to be needed.

"Hungry yet?"

Chris's question dragged him out of his turbulent thoughts. "Not yet."

"Me neither."

Jamie swallowed slowly. Honestly, he was exhausted. Should he... Chris hadn't told him no yet. He was just waiting for it to happen. "Is it okay if I lie down for a while?"

"Oh, sure. However long you want."

Jamie put another foot between them. Every time he looked up, he felt himself leaning toward Chris. There was something in his eyes, in his voice, that Jamie couldn't resist. *Has to be because I'm tired.*

"Thanks," he whispered before spinning and fleeing for the bedroom.

He leaned against the closed bedroom door, panting. Flat palms to the door while the rest of him was so tense, his knees knocked. What was going on with him? He closed his eyes, desperate for air, swallowing thickly twice. Chris hadn't tried to touch him, hadn't crowded him, not once. He wasn't poking and prodding, demanding Jamie's secrets.

Jamie couldn't help the shivers. The only time his father had been this nice was right before he wanted money. The only time he'd acted like a father was right before he assumed Jamie was a bank and would forcefully withdraw if Jamie wasn't fast enough to give him what he wanted.

He slid down the door to the floor, gasping, fighting against himself to not be loud. He wasn't sure what was driving him, or what had snapped, but suddenly his chest ached and no matter how hard he pinched his eyes closed, he couldn't stop the tears. Why had he stayed for so long? Why had he never tried to leave before now? Why did it take the threat of being killed to force him into a no-win position?

A light tap on the door startled him. "Jamie?"

He sucked air, unable to hide the sob behind it. "Yeah?"

"Hey... Can I come in?" Chris was using that soothing voice again. Shame washed over him. Jamie hadn't been able to hide his meltdown.

Jamie felt if he told him no, Chris wouldn't push, wouldn't force his way in, but he didn't have the strength to fight him if it came to it. Slowly he slid across the floor, out of the doorway. The door cracked. Chris first looked at the bed, then sharply searched until he landed on Jamie.

"Jamie." He didn't say anything else. He fell to his knees, pushing the doorway wide. A trembling hand rose, but didn't touch. "How can I help?"

Jamie didn't have a single answer. It surprised him when Chris cautiously stretched out on the floor, leaning against the bed.

"It's going to sound crazy," Chris whispered. "But when I was younger, when I was having problems, my mom would sit with me. Would you like that?"

Jamie worked a burning throat, everything else in the room vanishing beyond Chris. Jerkily, he nodded.

Chris studied him for a few seconds, then settled in, apparently unconcerned that they were both sitting on the floor in the cramped space between the bed and the wall. He propped himself against the bed, resting his head on the edge, gazing up at nothing. "I can remember when Cade and Quade switched rooms, trying to fool her. They did it a few times, and she always knew."

Jamie scrubbed his eyes, tears still falling. The only way he could breathe was through burning gasps. Chris didn't pressure him to pull his shit together; rather he sat calmly with his hands clasped on his thighs. For the next hour at least, he sat and told story after story about the three of them growing up, about the pranks the twins used to play on not just their parents, but anybody who would fall for them. There were short tales about showing calves in the high school 4-H, about the way he just fell into his father's footsteps as a veterinarian, tagging along like a puppy even when he was a child. Stories about dogs and puppies, mud and horses, and a few calves that had to have their own way. Jamie wasn't sure if Chris was even aware of what he was saying, simply talking to fill the silence with the soothing cadence of his voice.

The man was gifted with that voice and the talent to use it to bring Jamie back from the edge he was clinging to with mental fingernails.

Slowly, the aching pressure in Jamie's chest relented and his eyelids drooped. He shook himself awake once, not trusting himself or Chris to fall asleep with him in the room.

At some point, he remembered Chris urging him off the floor, awake but drifting. Chris eased him onto the bed and covered him with the blankets he'd pushed out of the way for Jamie.

"Get some sleep, Jamie," he said.

Jamie thought he mumbled something, but between the days and nights he'd been dealing with the elements, the earlier food, and Chris's soothing voice, he was asleep before Chris closed the door behind him.

## Chapter Five

Chris looked at the clock on the stove. Jamie had been asleep for several hours. He'd even managed a few hours of a nap on the couch himself. Dinner was starting to sound like a welcome idea. He pulled two steaks out of the refrigerator, replacing them with two from the freezer to thaw overnight. Unwrapping the fresh ones to warm some on the counter, he washed up, then strolled to the spare room to check on Jamie. A light knock got no answer.

Carefully he cracked the door open. Fading light from the window illuminated the room well. Jamie was twisted up on the bed, shivering. Considering he was dressed like a grizzly in hibernation within his hoodie and under blankets, he shouldn't have been. He approached slowly, not wanting to startle him should he wake suddenly. When Chris stood over him, he noted one of the sleeves had bunched up and Jamie was holding his arm.

"Jamie?" He moved a little closer. There was sweat glistening on his brow. "Jamie? Wake up."

The man on the bed twitched and shivered.

Growing more worried and as carefully as he could, he touched fingers to Jamie's brow. "Shit," he hissed. He was scorching hot. He tried a little harder to wake him. "Jamie?" Chris shook his shoulder. Jamie rolled to his back, losing the hold on his arm. He moaned and trembled as his left arm shifted.

Chris walked around the bed and swept up the sleeve of his left arm. He cursed under his breath. It was swollen, an ugly red that was as unnatural as all the black and blue up and down the flesh, and there was substantial heat emanating off it. He'd completely missed it after Jamie's shower, absolutely overwhelmed with all the physical damage right out front. He carefully settled the arm to the bed, then pulled his phone from his pocket and called Quade direct.

"Dr. Rose."

"Are you still at the clinic?"

"Just finished the PM feedings. Why?"

"Turn the X-ray on. I'm bringing Jamie. I think he has a broken arm, and he's running a fever."

"Infection?"

"I wouldn't doubt it." Chris heard faint barks and yaps in the background as Quade moved through the building.

"Okay. Want me to set up the casting kit?"

"Yes. And thanks."

"No problem. Be careful."

They disconnected. The fun part was going to be convincing Jamie to go along with it.

Now it all more made sense, how he'd moved during the day, how he always held his arm close to his body. He'd barely used it earlier when they'd eaten lunch, in retrospect. Little signs that Chris should have picked up on and had missed. Unlike animals, humans could hide their pain if they were so willing. Chris didn't doubt Jamie had hid more than his share, and had been doing it for far longer than just the last few days.

"Jamie." Until he knew just how bad it was, he was going to treat him like spun glass. He shook a shoulder lightly. "Jamie? I need you to wake up."

Groggy, glassy blue eyes fluttered open. "What? Dad?" Chris almost wept when Jamie flinched into the bed. He was getting a clearer picture now.

"No, Jamie. It's Chris. Remember?"

"Am I late for work?"

*Definitely disoriented.* "No. You're sick. Do you remember today?"

Jamie's eyes closed, and he drew a shuddering breath. "Chris?"

"Yes. I need you to get up. Can you get up?"

"Where are my clothes?" Jamie pushed at the blanket, struggled, really.

"In the dryer."

"I need them." He was mumbling, rambling, as he tried to extricate himself to sit up.

"No, we're going to the doctor."

Jamie perched, panting, on the edge of the bed. Wild eyes were searching, bouncing around the room. He shook his head emphatically. "Need clothes if I have to leave."

Chris crooned, realizing he was making as much headway as he would with a drunk. "Not leaving. Just going for a drive, okay?"

Jamie clenched his arms around his middle, rocking, shaking with chills.

"Can you stand?"

Chris's suspicions were confirmed when Jamie used his right arm to push off the bed to reach wobbly feet, keeping his left tucked into his frame. He stuck out his own arm. "Here. Lean on me." He didn't want to risk a reaction by trying to prop him up.

It was a study in patience and coercion to nudge an unenthusiastic and distracted Jamie out of the bedroom all the way to the truck. Once he was inside and safely strapped down, he shut the door and jogged around the front. Jamie hadn't even realized he'd been barefoot on the paving stones.

Fifteen minutes later, he pulled up outside the clinic and honked his horn to get Quade to unlock the doors.

"Jamie?" He unlatched both buckles. "Jamie?"

Nothing.

Jamie was panting and sweating heavily, held up by the window glass.

Chris didn't waste another second, jumping from the truck to race to the other side. He opened the door and carefully rolled an unconscious Jamie into his arms, keeping the injured arm safely propped across his chest. The glass doors opened as he spun with his cargo.

"So glad you stayed late," he said in greeting.

Quade gave him an understanding smile, which was quickly replaced by a worried frown. "How long has he been like this?"

"I don't know. I was going to wake him up for dinner, and he was out of it. I looked at his arm. It's in bad shape."

"Okay. Put him on the X-ray table. We'll work with what we have. I've called Dr. Hoover for penicillin and antibiotics. He's on his way after a stop at the pharmacy."

"Thanks."

"Let's get this off him."

Together they stripped the hoodie and Chris felt his stomach twist at the signs of physical abuse on Jamie, now unavoidable under the bright ceiling lights. Quade's touch was gentle as he checked him from shoulder to wrist on both arms. "There's definitely something on his left. Better strip him down and do a full body exam."

Chris tried twice to get a reaction from Jamie, but he remained unresponsive.

Even Quade slowed in stunned anger as more and more became exposed. "He would have died had he remained with whoever did this," he informed Chris tightly.

"I know." Chris was also nearly positive without a doubt it had been Jamie's own father. A towel was splayed over his middle for the sake of modesty, and Quade went to work on the images.

A tap a little later on the front doors pulled them out of the mechanics of the X-ray process.

"Should be Dr. Hoover."

Chris nodded toward his brother and went to let him in. "Thanks for coming," he said in greeting to the man outside.

The man scooted through the doors, and Chris locked them behind him.

"Is he in bad shape?"

"He's been abused and is running a high fever. We both think he has a broken arm."

"Weak and injured. Not a good combination." Dr. Hoover's expression mirrored his own grim one. "Okay." He waved a hand to proceed, his medical carryall in the opposite one.

40

Chris led him to the back room, where Quade was still working over a naked Jamie. Chris stood to the side as Dr. Hoover joined him, shaking his balding head and *tsk*ing in concern and disappointment.

Chris answered the few questions he knew he could.

It turned out to be a long, worry-fraught night for Chris. His heart ached as much as his stomach, which clenched every time they found something that deepened his anger for the man who'd mistreated Jamie.

* * * *

"Okay, once he wakes up, these every four hours." Dr. Hoover held up a small bottle. "These every six for pain." Another bottle. "And these with every meal to help build his strength back up. All of them until they're gone."

Chris palmed them with a quick glance at the labels. *Good. Marked.* He'd never remember otherwise. "Thanks, Dr. Hoover. You're a miracle."

"Just remember, he's not going to heal like we do," Dr. Hoover advised from beneath bushy eyebrows.

For the first time since Chris was about thirteen, he blushed, avoiding the doctor's knowing gaze like he was still that horny teenager. Dr. Hoover gave him a kind pat on the shoulder and walked out the held door.

Quade snickered when he returned to the exam room. "Did he just bust you out?"

Chris cleared his throat. "Shut up," he growled. "I'm taking him home." They'd managed to redress Jamie into the loose jeans and T-shirt, but Chris refused to put the hoodie on him. It needed to be washed in such a bad way.

Once home, he spread Jamie carefully on the borrowed bed. Chris was still worried about the fever. Dr. Hoover had given him a shot and said the fever should start coming down within the hour. Covering him with the blankets, he put the arm with its fresh cast on top. It would likely confuse him when he first woke regardless. Hopefully he didn't knock himself on the head before he recognized what it was.

Chris spent the rest of the evening making and then eating dinner, though he had little desire to, and made regular checks on his guest. Eventually, Chris did notice a lessening in the heat that poured off him. He gave a sigh of relief knowing that Jamie was sleeping better now too. There was little doubt he needed that as much as everything else.

He leaned on the door frame, unashamedly watching over him, knowing he wouldn't be able to do it again for a while once Jamie was awake. It was no wonder Chris had thought he was younger at first. He was underweight, which emphasized his narrow frame. He had the most amazing blue eyes he'd ever seen, like stained glass; they were darker at the outer edge, then grew lighter inward. Pale and beautiful. It didn't bother Chris that he was slight and not overly tall. He'd never picked one way or the other when it came to large or small, short or tall. He just knew that when he found the right mate, all would be just what he wanted and needed.

Except he hadn't really thought it would be a nonshifter. That had caught him off-guard. Given the situation, he also knew he was going to need a gentle touch with Jamie. It had been several years since one of the pack had brought in an outsider. There truly weren't many in Silo, and even the ones who lived there tended to live in the outskirts. Only those who lived in a need-to-know environment knew they even existed. It was too dangerous to be ambivalent about their existence. No one person knew who they all were. It had saved the pack from pure annihilation more than once.

He sighed, crossing his arms as the old pang of emptiness swept up for his parents. Unfortunately, there were casualties. And there was no way to tell a wild from a shifter. A survivor usually did not live long after the death of their mate. A heart doesn't want to work when it is no longer complete. Once broken, they often follow in anguish after their mate.

His parents had been no exception. When his father had mysteriously been shot, his mother had overseen the burial, taken care of the legalities of passing on the clinic and house to their three sons, then had simply gone to bed one night and not awoken the next morning. It had taken Chris two years to make the home feel like he could live there without their ghosts haunting him, to make the house feel like his. It took another year to remodel their bedroom.

They never did find out what happened that night or who could have shot him. Since he'd been in form, everyone assumed it was an illegal hunter poaching on private property. Some still stalked the woods for the thrill, though as they were found they were either arrested or given the pack's brand of justice. Rarely did any dare return after meeting what they hunted face-to-face.

What the bottom line came down to was that he—all three of them—had lost both of their parents within a matter of weeks. Now he'd found Jamie and Chris was nervous, nearly terrified of screwing up something and chasing him away.

What if he can't understand? What if it's too much for him to accept? These were things he'd always thought he'd have time to talk to his dad about, and now he couldn't.

Straightening from the wall he reached and closed the door, letting Jamie rest. There wasn't anything he could do for him until he was awake, and one thing he did know he was going to do was take care of the young man. He had been gifted a great treasure in that sweet person lying unaware on the bed. Chris was going to cherish him, something that in and of itself was probably going to scare the shit out of Jamie.

# Chapter Six

It was about three in the morning when the screams woke Chris with the force of a cannon at his ear. He was out of bed and sprinting for the spare room. Chris threw open the door and found Jamie tearing up the bed like his life depended on escaping it.

"Jamie!" Chris shouted, sharp and penetrating. It seemed to snap him out of his nightmare. Chris turned on the light to show him he wasn't wherever the dream had taken him.

Jamie stuttered, shuddered, and collapsed onto the bed.

With cautious steps, Chris approached the bed. "Jamie? Jamie? Can you hear me?"

Thick, broken sobs were muffled by the pillow.

Chris ran light fingers through his hair. Jamie didn't respond, so he continued the light caresses while waiting for Jamie to focus. "It's okay. You're safe." Tremors rocked his frame like a hurricane shaking a small house. He repeated endlessly that Jamie was safe, waiting for something to bring him out of the mire his nightmare had dragged him into.

Slowly the sobs slowed to wet hiccups, and muscles unclenched across his torso.

"Jamie?" Chris tried again a few minutes later.

"Oh God," he moaned, hoarse and pain-filled.

"Shh. You're safe. It's okay."

Jamie shifted, and Chris stopped petting his hair. He faced Chris and sat stiffly on the bed. Chris sat too, nearer to his feet and out of reach, though his fingers itched to keep touching. "Okay now?"

Jamie looked at him wearily, then away. He nodded. He absently scrubbed at his face with a palm, wiping away tears.

"Want to tell me what happened?"

Jamie sagged, his head so low his chin touched his chest. He still sucked hard breaths, but he was calmer.

"I thought he was holding me down. I felt weight…" He raised the cast-covered arm. A dubious stare filled his flushed face. "Where did this come from?"

"You hit a high fever and were incoherent. Do you remember walking to the truck last night?"

Jamie shook his head.

"I am sorry for doing it without you knowing, but you were burning up." Chris sat with his hands on his lap. "I think your arm was causing an infection, and it finally caught up with you yesterday."

"My arm?" He was still listless and dazed. Lack of food and good sleep were also catching up with him.

Chris nodded. "You had a stress fracture across both bones. A doctor looked you over, and the cast was done. I have medicine for you." In truth, one more good knock or smack would have literally severed the minimal connection the bones still had.

His brow scrunched in confusion. "So…I went to the hospital?"

"I took you to the animal clinic. The closest hospital is over an hour away. We rely on two local doctors. Luckily, one of them is a family friend and wasn't against being dragged to the clinic to see you."

Jamie glanced up, then let his gaze fall faster than a stone. "Thank you," he whispered.

"Are you okay now?"

Jamie swallowed, but nodded yes.

"The doctor said to give you the antibiotics as soon as you woke up. Think you can?"

Jamie motioned that he could. He wasn't saying all that much, and Chris wasn't expecting it.

Chris knew it was a shock, all of this, not just waking up with his arm in a hard cast. "I'll be right back." He left Jamie to gather the first doses of medication and a tumbler of water. When he returned Chris told him, "You've been asleep since you laid down yesterday afternoon, not counting the fever. Roughly twelve hours."

"I feel like I could sleep for a week," he admitted.

"The toll of the fever." And the abuse. And the infection. And so many more things that he refused to burden Jamie with. They didn't need to be listed and reiterated. He watched Jamie take both pills and about two-thirds of the water. He probably wasn't even aware and had been enduring the fever for a lot longer than just yesterday. It made Chris doubly glad that he had found him because he didn't want to think what would have happened if Jamie had grown that sick while still out and alone.

By the time he was done with the water, his color was better and he was breathing normally.

"Get some rest."

Jamie didn't argue after handing back the glass. He burrowed under the blankets and bunched his pillow up.

Chris shut the door behind him. He closed his eyes and exhaled a shaky breath, feeling helpless to help Jamie. That nightmare had proven his suspicions behind who had been abusing Jamie. At least it was a person who would never get close to him again. Ever. A moment later, he made himself walk away from that door to leave the glass in the kitchen and find his own bed.

* * * *

Jamie stretched, freezing for a moment before recognizing the weight of the cast on his arm. Man, he must have *really* been out of it to not know about that. He laid out on his back, staring up at the ceiling. The room was brighter now with morning light. The sheets and blanket were pushed down, probably a reaction from the fever and nightmare. He was also still fully clothed.

Sitting up, he noticed there were clothes stacked on the dresser in front of the bed. They looked like his. Standing to investigate, he was surprised to find that they were. All the clothes he'd given to Chris the day before to wash.

It was a lot to accept. The medical help. The clothes. Being taken care of. And he still couldn't come to one idea of what Chris wanted from him. Looking for his backpack, he spotted it untouched by the door. Filled with trepidation, he went and opened it. His wallet was still in it, along with the nearly empty bottles of water and the trash of his previous meals, if protein and granola bars could be considered meals.

Flipping through the wallet, he counted the money. It was all still there, not that there was much. Thirteen dollars. It was all he had after paying the house bills and giving his dad extra gas money, though they both knew it wasn't going to make it into the car. He let the pack slip from his fingers to the floor with a nylon thud.

Taking a few minutes to adjust to working around the cast and the trapped fingers, he changed out of the clothes he'd slept in and dressed in his own. A trip to the bathroom offered yet another surprise. A shower pack with a fresh toothbrush and personal items.

It didn't have a bow on it or anything that obvious, but it was clearly left for him.

Jamie blinked rapidly to deter the rush of tears. A few deep breaths later and he was able to put the bathroom to good use; he felt as human as he could afterward, considering.

Staring at his reflection, he finally got a look at his face. The bruising was definitely fading around his jaw, no longer neon blue and purple, and it looked like his lip was well on its way to healing. He tilted his head, staring at himself. And then it hit him.

His hoodie was gone.

The view in front of him wavered. Jamie's stomach rolled. Braced on the sink, he drew air through his nose until it settled.

*Of course it is. They had to treat the arm, right? So that means...* He wasn't sure he was ready to face any more, but he couldn't avoid it. They knew. At least Chris did. Knew it wasn't just his face. Or just his arm.

And yet, he'd been nothing but gentle and patient. As though he didn't want to cause Jamie more pain or discomfort. The ache in his arm was considerably less, and he was feeling steadier. He stared hard at himself in the reflection. Everything was still a bleak blank hole in his life. He didn't have any more options than he'd had the day before.

Chris had only agreed to one night. Jamie wasn't going to press for more. He wasn't going to take a chance that all the goodwill he'd been receiving had a price he couldn't possibly pay.

Firming his shoulders, he opened the bathroom door and looked to either side, catching faint voices coming from the kitchen. Chris and Cade? He would have rather talked to him alone, but there wasn't any point in procrastinating over the inevitable. He stopped in the bedroom and cleaned up, straightened the bed, and then packed the remainder of his clean clothes in his backpack. He'd ask Chris if he could refill his water bottles before he left.

Done and standing, he looked around and realized his hoodie wasn't there. Chris probably knew where it was. It was all he had for protection. Gliding the pack onto a shoulder, he walked from the room.

The scent of fried bacon made his mouth water. Would Chris let him eat again?

"Morning, Jamie."

He blinked and focused on someone who for all purposes should have been Cade, only his hair was shorter.

The man stood from the kitchen table and offered a hand from the other side. "You probably don't remember last night, but I'm Quade."

*Cade's twin.* He shook, though it was brief. Just then, Chris came out of the laundry room.

"Morning," he said cheerily. "I just put your hoodie into the dryer." He stared at the backpack on his shoulder, a not-too-subtle disappointment in his expression. "You don't have to leave right this second, do you?"

Jamie worked his lip between his teeth. "No."

"Good. Breakfast is ready."

Obligated but not about to complain about being *made* to eat, Jamie let the pack slip to rest on a chair frame. He was glad to get to eat again, but the situation still made him wary.

"How do you feel?"

Jamie studied the other brother. He was exactly like Cade, less the tattoos and the longer hair. Same eyes and chin. "Better." But Jamie only had one direction to go after being at the bottom for so long.

Before he knew it, Chris had given him a glass of juice and three pills. "Take the pink one with your food. It's a high-dose multivitamin."

Jamie palmed them and realized he should have asked about the other two last night before he'd taken them. "And these?"

"Antibiotics and a time-release painkiller to give your body a chance to heal," he explained knowingly.

Jamie curled his fingers over the pills, unable to look up at either of the men in the kitchen. "You know." They'd seen everything.

"We had to, Jamie," Quade offered in a caring, professional tone. "You had an infection, and we needed to know if it was one or more broken bones. Did you know you had a cracked rib?"

He shook his head. With everything else, what was one more ache or pain?

"How many eggs?"

"Three," Quade answered.

Jamie blinked when he was prodded. "Jamie?"

"Um, two?"

"How do you like them?"

"Scrambled."

"Two tornadoes, coming up," Chris quipped, flipping his spatula. Jamie couldn't help himself, and his lips twitched.

Jamie swallowed the pills with several gulps of orange juice, licking his lips when he drained it dry. He giggled when he burped. "Sorry."

"No worries. You should hear him." Chris pointed the spatula at his brother.

What was funnier was Quade, with his subdued demeanor and calm exterior, didn't balk at the accusation. He looked almost...*proud* of it.

"More?" Quade already had the jug of juice out and propped, only waiting for Jamie's okay.

"Please," Jamie replied, trying to not fidget. He wasn't used to being waited on. His glass was filled, and Quade retook his seat. He was beginning to relax again being in their presence, neither one badgering him or pressing for answers, or really much of anything. And then...

"Chris says you need a job."

"What?" Jamie choked, covering his lips with a hand, trying to not confuse orange juice for oxygen and swallowing wrong.

"Master of subtlety," Chris rebuked him along with a glower. He continued working over a sizzling pan.

"Okay, okay," Quade grumbled. He faced Jamie. "The truth is, one of our part-time vet techs is going back to school. We need someone to take his place. It's a messy kind of job. Cleaning cages, walking animals, checking feeding requirements. It doesn't pay a lot, but it's steady work."

Jamie wanted to shrink down into his chair. "I can't."

"Why not?" Chris asked, puzzled. He placed plates of food on the table.

"I can't stay," Jamie whispered.

"If it's a place to live, you can stay here," Chris offered. "I'll charge you rent if that's what you want."

Jamie still avoided their gazes.

"Jamie." A chair scratched the floor, and Chris sat at his shoulder. "What are you running from?"

"Why are you being so nice?" he demanded right back, almost snarling as fear, hope, longing, and other emotions swamped him out of nowhere. He'd never met anyone like Chris. None of his friends, if they could even loosely be called that, had treated him so kindly. He had no other family. So why? "No one is nice for nothing."

Chris and Quade shared a shocked stare.

Chris bowed his head and then finally relented. He gazed up with nothing but truth. "Okay. I'll answer yours if you answer mine. What are you running from?"

## Chapter Seven

Chris stared into wide, frightened eyes. Jamie's lip trembled, and he bit it.

"I just don't want him to find me," Jamie finally whispered. "It was my paycheck that kept the house paid for, my money that he got drunk on day after day. He's going to want that back. In a bigger city, I won't be so easy to find. Once he realizes I'm really gone, he'll look for me." By his expression, Jamie was absolutely convinced of that.

Chris lifted a hand and gently, so very gently as to not startle him, touched Jamie's cheek. His heart thudded when those blue eyes blinked, but he didn't flinch enough to pull away. "He may look, he may even be lucky enough to find you here, but I can promise you he won't ever be allowed to hurt you again. We'll keep you safe. Give you a safe place to live, a job where no one can take what you earn away from you. Well, other than taxes, but I'm not a magician," he teased, trying almost desperately to crack through Jamie's fears and worries.

Jamie's confusion was palpable in his gaze, in the wringing of his hands on his lap. "Why are you doing this?"

Quade's deeper voice enfolded them both in caring arms from across the table. "Because we were taught to be givers, Jamie. Not takers. We give to our community. We give to our friends when they need us. We help when we can, and none of us were ever taught that it was okay to treat another, human or animal, the way you've been treated." Quade moved away from the table as though becoming aware that he was leaning close on his elbows. "Honestly, I *hope* he shows up. Only a coward beats up on a weaker person to prove that they themselves are not that weak. Jamie, you're so much stronger than your dad already."

"He always hated that I was so small. Couldn't do anything *manly*," he bitched bitterly. "I worked my ass off before I was even out of school because he was such a dick he couldn't hold a job. By the time I was twenty, I was taking care of everything."

"See?" Chris encouraged. "You're more than he'll ever see, more than he'll ever be."

Jamie swallowed, leaning just a hair into Chris's touch before pulling away. "I really do appreciate all you've done." He straightened and pinned Chris with a gaze that he swore he felt hit his spine. Time seemed to stand still for several heartbeats, then he heard, "He tried to kill me."

Chris had expected something, but not such a blunt explanation. He steadied himself for the answer he'd get to his next question. "Why?" he asked, absorbed and angered all over again. There was nothing else in his focus but Jamie.

Jamie swallowed, his pulse racing wildly beneath his skin. "I told him I'm gay."

Chris saw him hold his breath, awaiting the blow that he'd already lived through once. He saw the fear in his eyes for divulging the truth and recognized clearly the trust Jamie was granting to him that Chris wouldn't do anything like what his father had done.

"Okay."

*Three...two...*

"Just okay?" Jamie squeaked. Shocked tremors rocked his frame.

Chris caught it out of the corner of his eye when Quade raised his fisted hands to cover his mouth. He wasn't laughing, but there was clear relief and he was smiling.

"Jamie." Chris inched a fraction closer, not losing Jamie's gaze. Between just them. "I'm gay."

Jamie gasped so deep and hard, Chris was worried he was going to pass out. "But...but..." A disbelieving gaze bounced between Chris and Quade. "Quade?"

"No, and neither is Cade, but I can guarantee that Chris could still kick our asses if we had a problem with it. We don't. We love him the same as he does us."

"Do you see now, Jamie? You're safe here." Chris touched his cheek again, craving the closeness. "You're not alone, either."

Jamie's lashes swept low, and Chris's heart punched into his ribs. He'd never met a more sincere, tender person. Jamie's father had never known the wonderful man he had in his son. It appeared that Chris had stunned Jamie speechless.

He let his hand fall away from the warmth of Jamie's skin. "Now, we need to eat," Chris stated after the shock of silence had taken over for several minutes. Chris stood and finished gathering the rest of the food he'd been working on. No one complained that it had grown cold during their discussion. He was silently thrilled when he saw Jamie take his third pill after cleaning his plate and draining his glass one last time. Nothing would make him happier than seeing Jamie healthy, safe and happy.

At least now he had an honest chance at seeing that happen.

* * * *

They were finishing up when Quade's cell phone rang.

"Hello?" Jamie watched him grow very serious, his face troubled. "There was no damage to anything else? Did it look intentional?" He nodded to himself. "Okay. Yeah. We're done here at Chris's. I'll drive over there next. Make sure you get a police report regardless of whether they find something. Okay." He disconnected and looking up said, "Cade sent Lyla to throw out some trash, and the Dumpster had been set on fire."

Jamie frowned, watching both Chris and Quade.

"Is she okay?" Chris asked.

"Yeah. She ran in to call nine-one-one and got Cade to stand with her to watch for any issues."

"Why would someone do that?" Jamie held his hands on his lap, confused and equally troubled for them.

"That's the second time that's happened," Chris grumbled with deep annoyance. "The deputy blew it off the first time. There's no way this is just happening, like self-combustion. Or teenagers."

"Cade said he was going to take a very thorough look around the Dumpster and the parking lot. There has to be something there."

"Go ahead," Chris said. "We'll be right behind you."

They both said goodbye to Quade, then he was gone.

Jamie swiveled to gaze at Chris. "You want me to go with you?" Jamie asked, more than a little surprised to be included.

"Sure. It'll give you a chance to see the clinic. You can think about the tech spot."

"Quade was serious?"

Chris chuckled, shaking his head at him. "Of course he was."

Jamie twisted his hands. "Can I think about it?"

"Sure. Come on, let's get going."

Standing from his chair, Jamie spotted his backpack hanging on it. Chris seemed to be watching him, as though waiting for him to decide on the next step of his future. Was he willing to ignore the good fortune before him? Did he want to keep going, find a new city, with no friends, no place to be safe to go to?

Realizing he was being stupid and stubborn, he grasped the bag and carried it to the bedroom to leave on the bed.

Walking into the kitchen, he noticed the pleasure on Chris's face. That, more than anything, took him by surprise. *He wants me here.* He really didn't know what to think about that. Whatever he had been expecting, that hadn't been among them.

Jamie gripped the top of the chair he'd sat in. "Do you think my sweatshirt is dry?" He didn't mind now that Chris or Quade had seen his body's abuse but he wasn't comfortable being exposed, long sleeves or not. He knew his face was still showing too much of what had happened to him.

"Probably; let me grab it." He disappeared into the washroom, carrying it in his hand when he came out. He tossed it to Jamie across the table. "Good to go."

Jamie smiled. "Thanks." He slid it over his head. "By the way, do you mind if I call my old job?"

"No." He offered the cell phone out of his pocket.

"Thanks." He finagled it to get to the screen, then dialed the grocery store. Following Chris from the house, he waited as Chris locked the house up.

"Accounting, please," he said when someone answered on the other end.

"Please hold."

Jamie followed Chris to the truck and climbed in. "Accounting. This is Andrea."

"Hi, this is Jamie Ness. I wanted to apologize for my sudden disappearance from work. I had issues at home and had to leave suddenly."

"Jamie. Are you okay? Your father came in and said you'd been so sick."

Jamie developed a bad feeling from the news that his father had been to the grocery store. "I'm doing better," he offered weakly. He ran his hand down his leg, the cast making movements feel odd. "I was hoping I could get my last check forwarded to me."

"I'm sorry, Jamie. It's already been mailed to your home address from corporate. Your dad said you wouldn't be back and that you'd requested it."

*Crap.* Jamie managed to swallow the grumbled sigh. "That's okay. I am sorry, but no, I won't be back." Maybe his dad realized how badly he'd screwed everything up. Maybe, but he doubted it. He'd already managed to get Jamie's last check, so what was left?

"I'm sorry to hear that." There were a few more platitudes, but Jamie really didn't hear them. He disconnected the call numbly.

"Everything okay?" Chris asked as Jamie handed over the phone.

"My dad has my last check. It's as good as gone."

"Damn. That sucks."

Jamie agreed. He tucked his hands into the front pockets of his sweatshirt and watched the scenery go by in dejected silence.

"The offer still stands," Chris said quietly. "I'm not going to kick you out."

"You only agreed to one night," Jamie pointed out, not wanting to push his luck with the wind taken out of his sails over the money.

"How about one night at a time?" Chris replied with a smile. "I don't mind having a roommate. Remember? I have twin brothers. I'm used to noise and mayhem."

"I don't know," Jamie answered, sliding him a glance. "I'm pretty boring."

Chris winked at him but didn't argue. Jamie hunched into the seat. It didn't seem like he had a chance to win if he kept fighting about it, and really, what was he arguing against?

When they pulled up to the clinic, the fire truck was just leaving. Chris parked in a spot, and Jamie joined him on the asphalt when he got out. They walked to the rear of the building, where they found a police car, Quade and Cade, and a woman in a maroon tech uniform.

The air was sour with burned plastic, God-only-knew what else, water, and heat. The ground was flooded beneath the Dumpster. Jamie didn't see lingering tendrils coming out of it, so it looked like the firemen had done their job.

He and Chris stopped near the others in time to hear Cade finish the report. Cade had his hair restrained in a ponytail and wore a similar medical outfit as the young woman, but other than that he looked like the big, bruiser biker type that Jamie had met the day before. And an exact copy, less personality changes, to Quade.

There was an incredible resemblance between the three brothers. Chris's hair was a little darker brown and the twins' was a little more auburn, but they all had the same gray eyes. Standing next to them, even outsized, outweighed, and outnumbered, he didn't feel threatened by any of them with the way they circled around him. Studying them, he noticed that as soon as he and Chris joined the group the three brothers had moved closer, as though they were protecting him. From what, Jamie had no idea, but the realization shocked him. It took a few seconds, but right after that sank in he began to relax in a way he hadn't been able to since leaving home.

He *was* safe. And even more crazy, he was wanted. He rubbed an itch on his chin against his shoulder, catching a smirking smile from Chris. Jamie raised an eyebrow in question.

*Nothing,* Chris mouthed silently in answer, then refocused on what the deputy and Cade were discussing.

For the first time in almost a week, Jamie felt…happy.

It felt good.

## Chapter Eight

Chris waited as Jamie vanished around the corner with Lyla, asking questions about the clinic.

"So what do you think it was?" He waited for Cade to wash up and dry his hands on paper towels to throw away.

Quade leaned against a close wall, his expression mimicking his brother's thoughtful worrying. "Honestly, I have high doubts that it's kids. The last time wasn't a weekend, either. It was midweek, when everyone should have been at school or work."

"Was there anything unusual out there either time?" Chris asked. "Anything combustible by mistake?"

"No. I was working the last time, and there wasn't anything but the usual. Papers, office trash," Quade pointed out.

"How long ago was it?"

"Around Valentine's Day, I think," Quade told him.

"Right. You had a date that night, and were pissed it happened." Cade poked fun at his brother.

Quade rolled his eyes. "I'd tell you to grow up, but you're still the youngest."

"By three minutes," Cade retorted.

That was one argument Chris did not get into the middle of. Cade hated it whenever Quade played the older-brother card.

"Anyway," he said, redirecting them. There were only twenty months between him and the twins in truth, though they'd been separated by two full years of school. "Was there anything else that you remember about it, Quade?"

He grew silent, then said, "No. It just seemed so unusual to begin with."

"Do you remember who was working that day?" Chris waited as Quade thought about it.

"Lyla and Emily for sure. Allen. I think that was it."

"Was Zoe still working here then?" Chris couldn't remember.

"Nah. She left before the first of the year," Cade said.

Chris grumbled. "Did Deputy Dave say he'd do anything other than file the report?"

Cade shrugged. "What can he do? We don't have any evidence or ideas behind it."

Lyla stuck her head into the exam room. "Sorry to bother you, but your eleven o'clock is here, Cade. Mrs. Hampton and Precious."

All three of the boys shuddered. Lyla swallowed her laughter. "I'll tell her you'll be right out."

"Thanks," Cade muttered.

"Oh, the joys of Precious." Chris couldn't help laughing a little. He'd dodged a bullet to not have this weekend's Saturday shift. Precious was well known between the three of them. Sweet as sunshine for Mrs. Hampton, and a total demon on wheels for anyone else.

"I don't care what people say. Chihuahuas can bite *hard*," Cade grumbled.

"Try starting with a treat first," Quade offered, though he was also trying to not laugh, feigning sympathy for Cade.

"Asshole," Cade muttered. He left the other two to see to Precious.

"We should go look around out back and check the pens," Quade said.

Chris nodded just as a raucous round of laughter, high-pitched yaps, and squeals erupted out of the cage room.

Chris and Quade both hurried to go see what the commotion was. Chris was surprised to find Jamie on the floor, surrounded by a hoard of puppies, all of them trying to get onto his lap, lick him, or tug at his clothing with sharp puppy teeth.

"Help!" he crowed through his laughter. "I'm being puppied to death."

Lyla raced into the room and skidded to a stop, her hands on her hips to shake her head. Her stern expression was ruined by her swallowed giggles. "That's Mr. Thorne's hunting litter. They're here for their puppy shots."

"The whole herd?" Jamie asked, breathless. "How do you do it?" He lifted one, and the spot on his lap was immediately filled again.

"Usually one at a time," Chris said, attempting to unbury him. One by one, the pups were placed in the floor pen.

"Bye, guys," Jamie whispered, sticking his hand over the wall for a few last licks. "God, they're a mess." He stood up and dusted his clothes off. Then he ducked his head. Chris heard Lyla leave to answer the phone, Quade following her now that the rowdy canines were taken care of. "I was only going to pet one, but then they started crying and…" He lifted supplicating hands. "I couldn't leave any behind."

"It's okay, Jamie," Chris said, giving him a light rub to the shoulder. He snagged on unblinking blue eyes and felt his heart trip. Jamie was, in a word: cute. He carefully stroked a thumb over the discoloration on his jaw. "Does this still hurt?"

Jamie shook his head.

Chris didn't mean to but he slid upward, finding the plush smoothness of Jamie's bottom lip beneath the hunting stroke of his thumb. "Here?"

"No," Jamie whispered.

Chris had been very careful with how he approached Jamie. The younger man was scared and unsure. That caution didn't stop Chris from wanting to kiss him just the same. And now they were alone, not that Chris would hurt him. Far from it, but there wasn't anyone there to remind him to not want Jamie, either. Just like he couldn't help but watch him sleep, he couldn't help himself for feeling the way he was feeling with Jamie's skin in his palm.

It was the last thing he wanted to do, but Chris forced himself to let Jamie go and take a step away. Looking away, he drew a steadying breath and convinced himself to calm down and focus.

"We need to check outside for any signs of what or who was responsible for the fire."

"Okay," Jamie answered, that quiet note in his voice again. The vivaciousness he'd just witnessed from playing with the puppies was gone.

Chris widened the gap between them. He'd frightened Jamie, making him withdraw into himself. A state he hated even more so because Chris had put him there.

Twisting on a hard heel, he said, "Coming?" He didn't dare look to see if Jamie followed. He was likely to cradle him into his arms and never let go.

* * * *

Jamie stuffed his hands into the pockets of his hoodie. Silently, he followed Chris's clipped stride. He had no idea what he'd done just now to make Chris go cold.

He didn't seem angry about Jamie playing with the puppies. He stole a quick glance behind him to the pen to see them tumbling over one another, a soup of paws, tails, and ears. Cute little monsters. Jamie had never had a dog. His dad had never allowed one. When it sometimes had seemed hard to know how they were going to be fed, Jamie supposed a dog was out of the question.

So what had upset Chris? Trudging behind him out the rear door of the clinic, he just didn't know. He spotted Quade walking around the Dumpster, wearing a pair of latex gloves on his hands as he shifted stuff inside.

"Is it out?" Chris called when they were closer.

"Yeah. It's safe." Quade grimaced. "No idea what the plan was here, though."

"Well, let's see what we can find, if anything."

"Won't they come investigate it?" Jamie asked. He stayed a few paces away in case Chris took umbrage to his question.

"No. Unless there was damage or property loss, they don't investigate. This is considered incidental."

"Not arson?"

"Not unless we can prove it's intentional," Quade offered, shaking the Dumpster on its wheels. "Been through this once already." And it didn't look like he was any happier about it now, either.

"I'm going to check the horse pens," Chris said.

Jamie saw Quade wave him off as he continued to move around the Dumpster.

"Why the pens?" Jamie asked. "Did something happen to them?"

"No, but they're also back here, and someone could have tampered with them to cause us problems."

Jamie followed Chris up the short path to a squat brown shed. Chris unlocked the door with a key and poked his head inside. He came back out and locked it again. Jamie didn't get a good look inside but guessed it was storage of some sort for the outdoor areas.

After that, the first pen they came to was empty. Bins welded to the sides were empty. The second pen held two miniature donkeys.

"What are they here for?" They didn't look very happy, kind of listless and tired.

"They've been sick, so we've been pumping them full of antibiotics for the last three days.

They're here to not infect the rest of their home herd."

"Poor babies." Jamie stood by the fence and watched them for a moment. Jamie noticed that the same type of bins were welded to the sides of the steel pens. He guessed that was where they were fed or watered. Then he noticed something on the ground beneath one of the farthest bins. It was pale, but wasn't mud or grass. It looked... He tilted his head to make sure, and was sure he wasn't wrong. "Chris?"

"Hmm?" He tugged on locks without looking up.

"Is that a syringe?"

Chris snapped up so fast, it was a wonder he didn't crack his head on the steel pipes that made the pens. "Where?"

Jamie squinted, making sure he wasn't imagining things, then pointed. "On the ground, there." It just seemed like a really odd place to find one. Or lose one.

Chris slipped between two rails. The donkeys didn't so much as twitch as he walked past them.

"Quade!"

"Yeah!"

"I need a zipper bag."

"Is it?" Jamie asked, inching closer, but unable to get to that corner from the outside.

"Yeah." Chris sighed, running a hand over his head.

Quade showed up at Jamie's side. He stretched out an arm, giving Chris the bag. He inverted it and cupped the syringe to seal it up.

"Where'd that come from?" Quade asked.

"I wish I knew. We need to see if there's more." Chris looked toward Jamie and gave him a smile, the cool departure of earlier long gone. "Good eye, Jamie. I wasn't even thinking of something like this. I was worried about property damage."

Jamie ducked his head, unaccustomed to the praise. Together, the three of them combed the remainder of the pens and the shed area, but found nothing else.

"I wonder if this was what someone was burning in the Dumpster." Quade scratched his chin, a thoughtful expression on his face.

Chris faced him. "It's possible. Did you see any others?"

"No, but that doesn't mean they're not there." They started back up the walk to the pavement and the Dumpster. "Let me try again."

"Don't you just throw them in the Dumpster when they're used?"

"Can't. It's illegal. There are containers that we have to use, and they're picked up and then taken to a hazard waste site," Quade explained at Jamie's side.

"Oh." Jamie had no idea there were those kinds of safety rules for vets too. He'd heard about those kinds of regulations for hospitals and stuff. He guessed they all could be used given the right incentive, regardless of where they originated from.

"I'll call the deputy out to grab this for a drug test."

Jamie stood at Quade's shoulder as he sifted through the trash, Chris a couple feet away on his cell phone, reporting what they'd found.

"Okay, eagle eye. Let me know if you see anything," Quade said.

Jamie grinned, but didn't lose his focus just the same as he followed movement from a different angle. Clod after clod of garbage was shifted, raised, and moved.

"Wait!"

Quade froze. "What do you see?" Quade was trying to elevate from the outside enough to see from a different angle.

"Don't move anything." Jamie heaved himself over the wall and landed in the wet muck. With a hand on the Dumpster wall, he inched closer. "This is so gross," he muttered.

"Here." Chris shoved a pair of gloves at him.

Jamie slid one on his unencumbered hand. Using the toe of his sneaker, he hefted up some soggy, scorched papers. "Hold that." Quade grabbed the wad. Jamie wobbled as he stretched.

The strength of warm fingers on his anchoring hand whipped him up. Chris was staring at him, a strong hand holding him. "I got you." The contact surprised him, but it was the heat of his fingers and the depth of his voice that made his heart pound once or twice. Jamie couldn't pull away. Didn't want to. He truly believed Chris would hold him for anything at that moment.

He bobbed his head and then stretched beneath what Quade was keeping out of the way. "Do you have another one of those bags?"

Quade and Chris shuffled for a moment, then Chris handed him one. Jamie gathered his find the same way he'd seen Chris do it, removing the two mostly melted needles buried between things he didn't want to examine.

"Not sure how much they'll get from them." He handed them over. "Hold it just a minute more, Quade."

"You got it, boss," he quipped.

Jamie snickered as he dug a little deeper. "I think they were hidden in this." He pulled out a small tote, mostly burned through, but there were signs that the needles had been in it by the pattern of scorch marks and the damage the melting plastic had caused the nylon fabric itself.

"Do you see anything else?" Chris asked.

Jamie set the tote to the side on the pile and flipped through a few layers of garbage. "No."

"Okay. Let's get you out of there, and bag that up too, before Deputy Dave gets here." Chris's fingers squeezed his once, bringing Jamie closer.

Jamie stripped the glove and tossed it down into the trash, Quade doing the same after bagging the rest of their find. Chris stood by the Dumpster wall and when Jamie swung himself over, Chris caught him and lowered him to his feet. Jamie's hands landed naturally on strong shoulders.

Jamie's heart sped up that close to him, his breath hitching. The shocking thing was that the reaction wasn't out of fear.

"Thanks," he managed to say. Jamie's chest trembled standing that close to Chris.

"Anytime." Chris's fingers danced, holding him closer for just a heartbeat before letting him go. "Thanks for the help."

Jamie stood trapped by Chris's gray eyes. Unblinking windows that he couldn't escape.

He wasn't sure he wanted to. Or what it was supposed to mean.

## Chapter Nine

Jamie waited to the side as the brothers again gave information to the deputy along with the evidence they'd found. He stayed quiet with his hands in his front pockets. Every now and then, the cop looked his way and it made him want to flip the hood up on the sweatshirt and duck his head, but he didn't. There wasn't any reason he shouldn't be there.

Finally, he noticed Chris's gaze locked on him. He seemed to be answering questions again. Jamie dug his toe in the dirt, trying to look invisible.

"Ready to go get cleaned up?"

Jamie startled, skipping a half-step before realizing it was just Chris. "Uh, sure." The deputy car was pulling away, leaving.

"It's okay. Dave was just worried. Wanted to know what happened to you." He glided a light touch down Jamie's cheek. "Told him you wrestled a bear and won."

Jamie snorted. "A teddy bear, maybe," he mocked lightly.

"Hey, that was a mean teddy bear. I saw it."

That got Jamie to laugh. He fell into step with Chris to go inside and wash his hands.

"So what do you think of the clinic?" Chris asked once they were inside. "Like Quade said, it's not glamorous. You'll be sharing time with Emily. Allen is the one leaving for school."

"I like Lyla." He looked over his shoulder toward the puddle of puppies. "Will I get to play with the puppies?"

"When we have them, unless they can't, sure. The bigger animals usually just want a break and the outdoors. We usually have a few animals here for overnights, and there's the occasional bad injury and surgery, but one of us and Emily will handle those."

"So basically, I'll be the mop bucket for afterward." Jamie twisted on a hip, watching Chris's expressions, hiding his knowing grins as much as possible. Low man on the totem pole has to start...well, at the bottom.

"Didn't want to put you off on the idea, but yeah."

Jamie studied the clinic from a more serious point of view. It was clean and bright with a typical astringent, sterile, medicinal kind of smell. It wasn't too large: five or so separate rooms consisting of the business office, three exam rooms up front, and a waiting room. The surgical area was in the middle of everything, with more cages along those walls. He already knew that much from talking to Lyla and walking around with Chris.

"Decent pay?"

"Decent. Won't make you rich, but there's insurance if you want it."

"Wow. You're pretty small. How do you do that?"

"Cade's brain." Chris seemed proud of that fact.

That made Jamie chuckle under his breath. The job wasn't stocking shelves but it wasn't rocket science, either. And he was good with the dogs, and he could learn to deal with cats. He studied the area one more time, giving Chris a serious look before opening his mouth. "Okay."

Chris's smile was soft, but the gleam in his eyes was huge. It kind of stole Jamie's breath for a heartbeat or three.

"Great. I'll bring you in Monday to do the paperwork and get you set up. You can meet Joyce, our accountant, then."

They started to turn to leave the room when Jamie said, "I don't have money for uniforms."

"We can spot you an advance on your first check for those. You'll need uniforms, plus sturdy shoes. Stiller Springs will have what you need. The local shops here don't carry those kinds of clothes."

Jamie nodded, trusting that assessment. Chris would know what they have in his own town and just what he'd need.

He paused before entering the reception-slash-waiting area. "Thanks, Chris. For everything."

Chris twisted in the doorway and gazed down into his face. "You're welcome, but trust me, we need someone here as much as you needed this. There aren't many in Silo I trust to work for us. I grew up with too many of them," he finished in a conspirator's whisper. Jamie pinched his lips together to hide his bubbling snickers. Locking gazes, Chris added, "Exactly," by his ear, as though including Jamie in his secrets. Chris straightened at his shoulder. "Besides, I like you, and I trust my instincts. You'll be fine here."

Jamie almost floated as they said their goodbyes to leave.

* * * *

Chris let Jamie go shower once they were home again, after showing Jamie how to wrap his cast to keep it dry. He grabbed a bottle of water out of the fridge and then walked to the barn to make sure Tiberius and Biscuit had plenty of hay. He'd fed them their grain that morning, so checking on those two was just busywork to get him out of the house.

He had to put some distance between him and Jamie or he was going to throw his control out the window and kiss him.

Leaving the clinic, Jamie had glowed. Seeing Jamie so happy was making Chris melt on the inside. He *liked* seeing Jamie that happy. He also suspected it wasn't a very common situation for the other man.

Twenty-two and sometimes he just acted and seemed so much older than his years. Chris leaned on the fence to watch the horses, sipping on his water in thoughtful silence.

Jamie had fine features and hair that waved just a little to end in curls behind his ears. Chris touched his thumb and forefinger together, remembering the brief seconds of contact from earlier when he'd tested Jamie's bottom lip. He was healing, just slowly. If Chris knew how, he'd take away all his pain. Jamie had seen too much pain in his life. He wished he could give Jamie his ability to heal. It didn't make it hurt less, just would help Jamie to heal faster.

Chris sighed and leaned on his bent arms on the top fence rail. He wasn't sure how he was going to go about *that*, either. Explaining *why* he could heal faster. Tiberius stopped on the opposite side of the fence and rubbed his chin in greeting over the top of Chris's head.

He grunted, closing his eyes, getting the equivalent of a horsey hug. "Sorry, no carrots today." He forgot to bring a couple with him when he came outside. Proof that his brain was occupied. Chris drew a breath. "How do I tell him, Bear?" he murmured, using the town kids' nickname for the lamb in a Clydesdale's body.

Jamie had been there barely more than twenty-four hours. Amazing, really, when Chris thought about it. He was adjusting and rolling with the punches, playing the cards life was dealing him. From being chased out of his home and being homeless to having a place to stay and a job. Chris wouldn't have done anything differently. Regardless of his wolf's desire, he *was* that type of person.

Quade was right. They had been raised to be compassionate to others. Even if Jamie hadn't been a miracle of fate for him... If Chris hadn't been drawn to him... He controlled the compulsive wave of desire that struck fast and hard, not wanting to rile his inner beast with Jamie inside and probably naked...and wet...

Chris groaned, feeling heat surge through his blood. A few long, deep breaths, and he had it under control again. That man was going to drive Chris crazy at this rate.

Even if Jamie *hadn't* been someone special to Chris, he would have made sure he was safe.

He knew life wasn't always fair, but it didn't help him understand the kind of people like Jamie's dad who lived on this Earth. There was something cruel and bitter in a person like that and taking it out on a defenseless person, likely since a point in his young life when he'd held no chance to fight against it or know he didn't have to live like that, killed Chris. He was just thankful that he'd finally found the strength, or even felt enough fear, to get out of it.

He was drawn to Jamie in ways no other man, no other boyfriend, had pulled at him. He was still getting to know Jamie, and he knew Jamie was still feeling his way through things. And Chris needed to use patience he didn't know he had.

He patted Tiberius's big head, scratching up over an ear. "Big dog, that's all you are," he crooned. Tiberius didn't seem to care one bit what was said so long as Chris didn't stop scratching. He smiled, well aware of the horse's good spoiling spots.

A few minutes later he twisted around at the sound of a vehicle, but wasn't expecting the yellow topless Jeep as it cleared the side of the house to stop in front of the barn. Ed raised his sunglasses to the top of his head before swinging out of the stopped vehicle.

"Hi," he said in tentative greeting.

"Hey, Ed. What's up?" Chris turned and braced his elbows on the fence to watch his ex walk toward him. They were done, but Chris wasn't against looking. Ed was more Cade's size, tall and broad like Chris. Short, buzzed hair and deep brown eyes that sizzled when he was lost in his passion. He was a man to want. Only Chris had let him go and didn't want him back.

There weren't many gay men in Silo, or even in Stiller Springs. He knew Ed had hoped things would go further than they had, but Chris hadn't been able to commit to Ed like that. He wouldn't lie to him, either. They both deserved better than half a relationship, and now that Chris had found Jamie he knew he hadn't been wrong.

He felt less now for Ed than he had when they'd finally called things off.

"Thought I'd see if you were free for tonight," Ed said nonchalantly, resting on an elbow beside him. He ran a teasing finger over Chris's shoulder. Heated interest sparked to life in brown eyes. The blatant flirting made Chris shy away a fraction. He didn't want to lead Ed into a misconstrued idea.

"Not happening, man."

"Why not? You're not seeing anyone. I'm free."

"Ed," Chris said with a groan. He slugged some of his water.

"Still sin on legs," Ed purred, moving closer to try to nuzzle his throat. Chris bunched his shoulder and moved away.

Ed sighed. "So it's like that, huh? Neither of us are tied down, and you won't even play?"

"I'm not tied down, but I have my eye on someone and I can't fuck it up," Chris told him.

"Who?"

"Not important to you," Chris chided in answer.

"Oh, ouch." Ed winced. He flipped and leaned against the fence, crossing his arms over his chest. "Not even for old times' sake?"

"Sorry, buddy."

Ed looked away. "Is he that good?" he asked, obviously pouting.

Chris glared at Ed.

He thrust up his hands. "Just checking. Got to see if I have any kind of chance here."

"None."

"Damn. Double ouch."

Chris smirked.

"I'm tired of being alone," Ed finally grumbled. "There's no one here."

Chris knew that. Couldn't change it. He was about to say something when Ed interrupted him.

"Wow," Ed said, moaning. "Where did he come from? He's beautiful."

Chris focused toward the house and spotted Jamie walking out the back door. He forced his voice into a neutral zone. He didn't want to alarm Jamie if he could hear anything they said.

"That's Jamie. My roommate for now. He had some trouble, and I found him."

Ed rolled a knowing glance over his shoulder. "Always helping the strays."

"Not a bad habit to have," Chris pointed out. Some of the Rose boys' quirks were well known.

"What happened to him?"

"Bad home situation." Chris wanted to hold out a hand and bring Jamie into his body as he drew near, but instead stayed still. Chris also noticed that Jamie wasn't wearing his hoodie. He was finally growing comfortable enough to leave that shell of armor behind. Maybe the taste in shirts would be next. It was all progress and he was happy for him, happy to see it. Now if he could get Ed to leave...

He definitely didn't like the way Ed was drooling over Jamie.

## Chapter Ten

Jamie eyed the man next to Chris cautiously. He thought he'd seen them talking rather closely before coming out, but now he wasn't sure what the story was between them as they just stood there. He slid a hand into a jeans pocket, unable to do much with the plaster-cast arm.

Tiberius was standing at Chris's shoulder, looking half-asleep.

"Sorry to interrupt," he said, shrinking between his shoulders.

"No problem." Chris smiled for him. "What did you need?"

"I was…" He took a slow breath. He wished he was more comfortable, but he didn't know the parameters he had to work with. No one had said anything about rules to him. "I was hungry and wanted to see if it was okay if I made some lunch."

"Oh, sure. Your house now, Jamie."

Jamie caught it when the other guy gave a nudge to Chris's side. Chris rolled his eyes.

"Jamie, this is Ed."

Ed put out a hand. "Nice to meet you."

Jamie swallowed and hesitantly let him take his hand. The grip was firm, but not hard, not crushing for all the muscle. It surprised him, but what made him almost gasp was the stroke of his thumb over skin before releasing Jamie's hand. He kept his gaze lowered.

"Um, okay," he replied, stuffing his hand into his pocket again. Where it was safe. "Did you want me to make something for you, Chris?"

"If you want. *Only* if you want," Chris reiterated. "I don't expect you to wait on me."

Jamie swung to latch on to Chris's gaze. There was patience and kindness there, just like there had been since the first minute he'd stopped beside Jamie on the road the day before.

"Okay," he offered quietly. "I need to take my medication." It wasn't really intended as anything more than filler for the silence, so he wasn't expecting it when Chris pulled out his phone to check the time.

"You're right." He turned to Ed. "I'll talk to you later."

Ed seemed taken aback, jerking a smidge and blinking at Chris. "Oh, sure. Sure." He took a step away from the fence where they'd both been propped. "Okay. Nice meeting you, Jamie."

Jamie nodded once, then watched Ed climb into the yellow Jeep. He turned the vehicle around and vanished around the house.

"I owe you one," Chris muttered.

"I'm sorry?" What did he do?

Chris smiled, swinging an arm over Jamie's shoulders in camaraderie. "I was trying to think of how to get him to leave without hurting his feelings. Don't worry. He's big, but he's harmless."

"Seems a lot of you Silo men are like that," Jamie returned, giving Chris a cheeky grin. "What do they feed you here? Obviously I wasn't getting it."

Chris gave him a gentle shake. "Quit. You're perfect." He released Jamie to open the door for them.

"*Bullshit*." Jamie coughed, his hand fisted in front of his mouth to prove it was a real cough. Sort of.

Chris ruffled his hair in blatant disagreement. "Keep trying. Not buying it. Let's go see what there is for lunch, and plan dinner."

"Okay."

\* \* \* \*

Jamie was nervous walking in to speak to Joyce first thing Monday morning, his stomach cinching a little with knots. She was a smiling black lady that obviously didn't know Mondays were evil. Though she didn't wear a suit, there was a certain air about her that spoke of experience and knowledge, even though she wore jeans and a plain top. Long tresses of permed hair were tied in a dark red ribbon. In many ways, she reminded Jamie of Lyla. Confident, kind, and compassionate, which helped him immensely to get over his nervousness during the first few minutes.

"Let's see here. I need these filled out, your tax info, insurance, application." She rattled off the particulars, what was expected for hours, lunch, and breaks, while she dug through papers on her desk. "I think that's it. And make sure I get the info on how you want to be paid."

He shrugged. "I guess in cash. I don't think people take goats anymore, do they?" Jamie asked with a straight face.

Joyce gave him a blank look and then burst out laughing. "Dang. I knew Chris was giving me another troublemaker." She wagged a finger at him. "I'll have you know, all troublemakers…" She leaned across the desk to impart her wisdom privately. "Only come in second to me." Joyce winked.

Jamie joined her with his laughter, glad she hadn't taken offense to his teasing, then took the documents to the break room to fill out. Finished, he returned them to her. "What do I do about hours?"

"There's a clock in the break room. Get yourself a card and put your name on it. Write in your start time for today at nine this morning, and then use the clock from here on after into eternity. There's a calendar in the break room. You need time off, you get it approved and write it down there. There's a ninety-day probation before you can do that, though."

"That's fine. So where do I start?"

"Go meet up with Emily and Allen. They'll show you the ropes. And welcome to the family, Jamie." She gave him a full-wattage smile that didn't seem faked in the least.

"Thanks," he replied, ready to go start his new job. He walked out with a bounce in his step. Things were definitely beginning to look up.

\* \* \* \*

Jamie hummed as he disinfected another cage. The Border Collie two cages down was nosing the gate, looking for sympathy. Jamie crooned for the poor boy. He was coming out of his anesthesia and not too happy. Not that Jamie blamed him. Toby had come in a stud and was going home a eunuch. At least he was too young to miss it.

"Hey, Jamie. I'm going to Mabel's to get tacos for lunch. Want anything?"

Jamie twisted to look at Emily in the cage room doorway. "Sure. How much?"

"Doc's treat."

*Even better.* "Cool. Anything but onions."

"Got it." She twirled and hopped out of view. Jamie had been there two weeks so far and was loving it. Chris, Cade, and Quade were all easy to work for, and as they rotated the clinic responsibilities between them, Jamie was learning their quirks.

Quade was by far the most clinical, always explaining every step and situation so even Jamie, who didn't know a single fact about veterinary medicine, could keep up. Cade was direct without being rude, and Chris was simply Chris. He didn't demand more than Jamie could handle and was willing to show him the ropes as they went along.

Chris had driven him to Stiller Springs during his first week to get clothes and uniforms for work. Jamie had tried to argue as Chris kept dropping stuff in the basket. He didn't know how much his check was going to be and could just see it vanishing as jeans, shirts, and uniforms were dropped together. Even undergarments. Then shoes. Then personal items.

It hadn't mattered. Before he knew it they'd paid, Chris had signed the slip, and they were walking out.

"I didn't even see how much it was," Jamie complained. How was he supposed to pay Chris back if he didn't know how much he'd spent? Both their hands were full as they aimed for Chris's truck in the parking lot. He knew it hadn't been a cheap trip.

"That's okay. I have the receipt."

Except Chris had yet to give him the receipt and the last time Jamie had asked, Chris said he'd lost it. Somehow, he doubted that.

He finished wiping down the cage he'd been working on and closed the door.

"Hey, uh, Jamie."

He glanced over a shoulder. Lyla stood there looking a little queasy. "Yeah?"

"Deputy Hanlon is here to see you."

"Me?"

She only nodded and then scurried away.

He wondered what that was about. He didn't have any outstanding tickets, he hadn't ever been arrested. He'd rarely driven since his dad had needed the car for his own use. Dropping the rag in the cleaning catchall, he rose to his feet and walked to the front.

"Jamie Ness?"

"Yes." An uneasy loss of equilibrium was bearing down on him staring at that uniform and the man in it, who was then staring at *him* in a cold, predatory manner.

"I need to ask you a few questions."

"Okay. Why don't you come back here?" Jamie faced Lyla. "Where's Chris?"

"With a patient," Lyla answered, worry apparent in her eyes.

"Let him know when he comes out, okay?"

She nodded.

Not willing to look behind him, Jamie led Deputy Dave Hanlon to the cage room for some privacy. "What can I do for you?"

He took out a notebook. "Just a couple questions. We had a report show up, and you fit the description."

Jamie swallowed. "Okay," he barely managed.

They covered a few basics: his age, his previous address, previous job.

"What's this all about?"

"Mr. Ness has filed assault charges."

Jamie stumbled and reached out for the closest cage. "But...but he tried to kill me," he choked out, panic rising swiftly to make his world spin. "He's the reason I have this!" He wrenched the cast-encased arm into the air.

"So it was self-defense?"

"What's going on in here?" Chris asked coolly, joining them. He came and stood at Jamie's shoulder. There was no sign of any kind of welcome on his face for the deputy this time.

"Clive Ness pressed assault charges against Jamie. The report said he was hit over the head and then robbed."

Jamie felt dizziness swoop in as all the blood drained from his face. "No. I was asleep. He pulled me from my bed and then beat me. I took what was in my backpack the day Chris found me and that was it. And it was all mine. Clothes."

"What is he saying Jamie stole?" Chris icily demanded. "He kicked Jamie out in the middle of the night. He also confiscated Jamie's last paycheck. If anything, he should have charges against him for stealing wages."

"Is that true, Jamie?" Deputy Dave's pen had stalled, his attention sharp.

Jamie nodded. "I never had a chance of getting it. He claimed it in my place, falsely."

Dave clicked his pen closed, his lips pinching for a moment. Then he slid it all into his front pocket. "Thank you both. If you see or hear of this person that this gentleman is looking for, just let us know."

"Thanks, Dave." Chris held out his hand, and they shook.

"Not a problem. Sorry to bother you. I'll let them know this is a dead end here."

Jamie watched him until his brown uniform was gone, then sagged. Chris's arms were strong, keeping him from sliding all the way to the floor.

"Come with me," he whispered close to Jamie's ear.

Numbly, he followed Chris around the corner for the private offices. Neither said anything until the door was closed to the outside world, then Jamie went limp against Chris's chest.

He moaned, a whimper of fear and pain.

"Shh. It's okay," Chris said in a soothing voice. He propped himself against the desk and enfolded Jamie into his arms. "He can't hurt you here. Dave knows perfectly well in what condition you arrived in Silo."

"I did hit him though." He gasped, trying to breathe, aware he was trembling but unable to stop. It was the only chance Jamie had that night to escape, one trophy. It was the only thing heavy enough to use as a weapon. He didn't regret it then and refused to now.

"Self-defense, Jamie. No matter what you did, you did it to get away." Chris's warm lips caressed his temple while tender, slow-moving hands stroked Jamie's spine at the same time.

It took Jamie several minutes to realize he was flushed completely against Chris, buried into his chest, clinging with all his strength, but neither Chris nor Jamie was in a hurry to separate.

"You know I didn't steal anything," Jamie whispered.

"I know you didn't." He nuzzled the top of Jamie's head.

Jamie's eyes remained closed, soaking up the contact. Over the last couple of weeks, Chris had become a really good friend. Someone Jamie was beginning to trust, and both Cade and Quade treated him the same, with kindness. Like he was part of their family.

He and Chris shared the house, cooked together, cleaned, whatever needed to be done, like a team. A closeness Jamie hadn't shared with his own father. His dad had relied on him first, which gave Jamie very little time for himself. Now he had that time and was enjoying doing things with Chris or around the house because he wanted to, not because if he didn't do them, they wouldn't get done.

Sundays were even better because all three of the brothers would converge on a house and they'd spend the day hanging out, cooking, and doing things together, again proving their closeness and caring for one another. At first Jamie wasn't sure how he'd fit into that mix, but they'd made room for him and he was learning to look forward to those days. So far, they'd met at Cade's to work on home improvements, bringing a whole new set of skills to Jamie as they taught him how to use power tools and build things. They never once treated him like he was some girly wimp. Quade had even teased him once about being the size he was as an advantage because he could scurry between roof beams like a monkey, squeezing into areas where they couldn't.

Jamie sighed, noticing how much more relaxed he felt now after being held for just a few minutes. The ordeal with Deputy Dave had made him nauseated and shook him up, but he was stronger now. He was beginning to believe he was safe too.

"Better?" Chris murmured. Warm breath ruffled Jamie's hair.

Jamie wanted to burrow deeper into the strong-armed embrace and stay there all day but knew he shouldn't. It felt so good to have someone he could turn to, someone who understood. He couldn't resist giving a squeeze regardless.

A gentle palm cupped his chin and eased him upward in answer. "Jamie?"

He sucked a short breath, unprepared for the sexy rumble in Chris's voice. Jamie had never heard it. Something he couldn't remember ever knowing made him feel hot and achy with a sudden flash of weakness. Chris's touch was sizzling skin, where he cupped his chin and his heart tripped in response. His world tilted as everything surrounding them vanished, leaving just the two of them.

Then Jamie did the unthinkable. He arched up onto his toes to brush their lips together.

## Chapter Eleven

Chris wasn't prepared for Jamie's kiss. Not physically, and not mentally. In a single brush of flesh, Jamie unilaterally derailed his control off the tracks of good intentions completely. He definitely hadn't expected him to make the first move.

Lashes fluttered as a red heat swamped Jamie's cheeks. "Oh shit! Chris." Jamie tried to wriggle away but Chris was still holding him, his hands splayed gently on his spine. Jamie tore his arms from around Chris's waist, letting them hang limp at his sides. "I'm sorry." Jamie's lashes fell like weights, hiding his eyes.

Chris threaded upward into the beautiful strands on Jamie's head and held him captive. "My turn," he said in a growl. His other arm remained locked around him, keeping him pinned body to body, angle to angle. Chris loved every second.

Jamie gulped, his gaze shooting wide. Whatever Jamie had expected, it wasn't Chris wanting him in return. Chris had been waiting weeks for the opportunity to taste Jamie's lips. Waiting for him to heal. Waiting for him to feel secure. Waiting for him to go after what he wanted with more confidence. Waiting that had nearly killed him and had his wolf pacing impatiently on more than one occasion. As each day had passed, Jamie was smiling more, laughing and joking, leaving the shell of his previous life behind. He still wore the long-sleeved shirts, but the hoodie had become a thing of the past. Except for the cast, he was nearly one hundred percent healed. He was one of the sweetest, sexiest guys Chris had ever known.

Holding him steady, he moved slowly enough that if Jamie wanted him to stop, he would. A word, a flinch, a sign. There was none.

Instead Jamie tipped, going pliant in Chris's palm as they neared. Desire raged through Chris's blood, racing to his heart and his dick. The first pounded erratically in anticipation. The latter ached and throbbed with its own pulse.

The first caress was gentle, a whisper of skin and breath. Chris was determined to not overwhelm him, or else die trying to maintain that control. Chris brought them together, and parts of his body trembled. Shivers of ecstasy riffled across his chest. Unsure how hard to push he forced himself to keep it light, but Jamie seemed to have other ideas.

Now that the line of untouchable had been breached, he slipped a hand behind Chris's neck, clutching to bring them even tighter together.

Jamie moaned hungrily and Chris answered, striving to give him what he needed. Thrusting to tease between his lips. What started as a tender, learning taste became a dueling battle with harsh puffs of air as they pushed and tugged for dominance against each other. Jamie melted into Chris's front, a natural melding of two forms. Blood echoed behind Chris's ears, hollow beats that kept pace with his erratic heart.

Taking a firmer control, Chris eased the kiss, softened it to finally release Jamie. Neither was in a rush to put space between them.

"Wow," Jamie whispered. He nestled beneath Chris's chin, both content to stay where they were. Chris was pretty sure Jamie was partially hiding and wasn't going to pressure him to do more than he was ready for, even at this point. "Glad you're not mad."

"Not mad," Chris replied. *Not mad in the least.* That passionate kiss proved that Jamie was drawn to Chris much the same way he was to Jamie. He nosed into the hair at his temple, taking in his body's heat and saving the scent of skin to be savored later. "But we should get out there." Even though he seriously didn't want to let the man in his arms go. Chris would be happy to hide from the rest of the world. And probably could be too easily convinced at that.

Chris felt Jamie's reluctance as he nodded. Jamie tilted to look up at Chris. "Will I have to worry about Deputy Dave?"

"Doubt it. One thing you'll learn is that we protect our own."

"But—"

Chris gently cut him off with a sipped kiss. "Yes, you are. I don't know what's going to happen here, but you *do* belong." Chris was perfectly aware of what he wanted to see happen but it was too soon to throw that at Jamie, and there were still other things that would have to be explained. He really wasn't looking forward to that. But when it came to Jamie's safety, that was as good as written in stone.

A knock on the door was followed by, "Lunch!"

"Coming," Chris replied. He straightened, though it was beyond reluctantly. The smile Jamie gave him when he stood to release Chris was worth everything. Chris drew a slow breath and exhaled it, hiding the groan when Jamie passed through the office door. *Too sexy, even in what should be an utterly unattractive uniform.* Too bad his libido wasn't listening.

\* \* \* \*

Jamie grabbed three tacos, a drink, and a few napkins, then snuck away before he could be snagged into hanging out with Lyla and Emily. Easing open the rear door of the building, he aimed for the picnic table on the farthest side of the rear lot, under a sprawling oak tree. It was far enough away from the pens and Dumpster to mostly forget they were there. Not perfect, but enough. He needed a few minutes away from what just happened to get his head on straight after that faux pas in the office.

Sitting to lean on an elbow to hold his chin, he picked at the tacos. He should be starving. Except... He'd just kissed Chris!

*Holy shit, what were you thinking?* It was a silent scream, and he winced at his own conscience's berating. Popping a chunk of tomato between his lips, he gnawed on the end of his finger.

Jamie just remembered looking up at Chris's profile and reaching. It hadn't been a deliberate action. It just...happened. He groaned, rubbing his face roughly. Of course Chris would kiss him after that invitation!

*But he didn't have to.*

Jamie straightened on the bench seat. "He wanted to," he whispered, just as stunned as he'd been at his own blunt behavior. He could have just as easily pushed Jamie away in any manner— disgust, anger, impatience. Yet he hadn't. Jamie had kissed a few guys. Embarrassingly, he was twenty-two and still mostly a virgin. He hadn't wanted anyone to see the marks on his body. He knew he wasn't perfect. Short, slight, almost pretty, depending on who he asked. He sighed, digging a finger into his food. Food he should be eating instead of playing with.

Now he was even more confused than he had been in weeks. He hadn't realized until their kiss that what he was feeling for Chris was more than friendship borne from kindness. He was actually attracted to the man. Jamie cupped his forehead and hunched over the table, blind to everything else around him, wallowing in the conundrum of his own making. The cast on his arm dragged over the table as he flipped through bits on the napkins, occasionally managing nibbles between his lips.

Replaying those few minutes between Jamie's kiss and Chris's, his world had once again been tossed on its ear. Was Chris going to tell him to leave now? What would Chris do?

He hadn't acted as though he wanted Jamie to leave but it was possible that would come later, when there wasn't a backlash from doing it there at the clinic. Jamie's stomach tossed at the thought, swirling with worry that he'd just screwed everything up and he'd be forced out again. He didn't believe Chris was the kind, but it was hard to assume it wouldn't happen. Taking faith that he hadn't messed up a good deal, a place to live and a new job that he was comfortable in, was a stretch after everything he'd already been through.

With a forced effort, he managed to finish his lunch. It was a hard lump that sat in his stomach for hours afterward fearing what would happen at the end of the day.

Whether it was deliberate or not, Jamie didn't see Chris for the rest of the afternoon. He tried to tell himself that it wasn't a problem, that it wasn't because of him, but because they were busy, as he was learning Fridays could be.

On top of the worries he had caused with Chris, he was even more confused and nervous over why his father had pressed charges. Was he looking for Jamie? Was he seriously determined to see him arrested? Had he really gone to the police or was it all a ploy to flush him out? Jamie had no idea. All the guessing did was add to his already anxious nervousness of the day.

In replaying all that happened the night they'd fought, Jamie was positive he hadn't hurt his dad enough to cause serious harm. He'd been more drunk than injured.

As the afternoon dragged on, the only thing he'd convinced himself of was that there was nothing he could do about his dad and hopefully some way he could fix everything between himself and Chris. Jamie didn't want to leave, didn't want to be ousted.

By quitting time, he was ready to beg.

\* \* \* \*

Chris waved to Lyla and locked the clinic front door behind her. He rolled his shoulders, trying to ease the tension that had been building through the afternoon. He'd purposely swung a wide berth around Jamie. He'd never known how hard it would be to not touch him now that he had. Had never known the craving he would be haunted by when it came to his kiss. This went well beyond a simple desire. His wolf had been impatient but biddable since they'd met. That was no longer the case. It was as though the control Chris had held over his inner beast had simply snapped like a dry twig under a heel. He growled and demanded, paced and snarled at every obstruction to be closer to the other man. He was making Chris's ears ring!

His wolf did *not* like being apart and out of sight of Jamie. Chris knew how to fix the problem, but he wasn't about to do that to Jamie, either. Not without full disclosure and Jamie's total understanding and agreement. It was life-altering being a were's mate, especially if said mate was human. Weres didn't exist in their world. Werewolves were creatures of fiction and occasionally of nightmares. Chris's wolf was all about instinct and survival and since that kiss he was clawing the shit out of Chris's subconscious to claim its mate, to keep them both safe and sane.

Chris snorted as the computer died for the night, the last processes a done deal.

Sanity had never been an option once a mate was located. He'd been playing with fire as it was with Jamie living under the same roof. The safety of the unknown and unconfirmed was officially obliterated, like the falling of the Berlin Wall. Gone.

"Shit," he grumbled, running a hand through his hair. And right at that moment it was only him and Jamie. Lyla was gone, Emily was gone. They had the PM feeding to complete and that was it. Then Quade would be back on duty the next morning for the Saturday half-day. Which meant Chris was back on night duty, and he was alone with Jamie for long stretches over the next seven days. It was going to be impossible to avoid him, except for when he was here at work and Chris wasn't.

He leaned on the desk before him on fisted knuckles, his head bowed, determined to do this right by the other man. Jamie hadn't had the securest upbringing, hadn't had a strong family to support him. He was confident, but his inner strength still had wounds that would take time to heal. Which meant no matter how badly he wanted to get naked and skin-to-skin with him, Chris was just going to have to cool his jets.

He winced when his wolf snapped at him. *Get over it.* The huff he alone heard was pure impatient derision. Chris could almost see the glow of watching eyes when he closed his own, his wolf was that close to the surface. Not a good balance.

When he felt he had at least a semblance of control, he straightened behind the reception counter and turned to start the evening feedings.

His gaze landed on a watchful and still Jamie, outlined by the door frame of the walkway to the rear rooms. All at once, Chris's heart surged while heat filled his veins. Jamie's pulse ticked with a matched pace, popping beneath the skin of his neck with an erratic beat.

Chris was moving before he knew it. Prowling before he could chain the need.

## Chapter Twelve

Jamie swallowed, a swift gush of breath shaking his body. "I wanted to say…I'm sorry," he whispered.

Chris's stride erased the distance between them in three paces. "What for?" he replied, hiding the raking hunger in his voice by trying not to say anything at all. *Primal.* Sheer need. This went beyond lust. Went eons beyond desire. Jamie was his.

Jamie took a faltering step, only to flatten against the closest wall. "For…for the kiss…earlier." Jamie licked his lip, his eyes jerking to the side and then dropping, hidden by dark gold lashes.

Chris raised an arm and blocked him with a flat palm over Jamie's shoulder. "You can't apologize for something I did," he stated.

Lashes whipped up, his blue eyes piercing with confusion.

"And you can't apologize now."

His brow furrowed. "Why?"

"Because I'm going to do it again," he warned Jamie.

A fine shiver tore over Jamie's smaller frame. Just like before, he gave Jamie the chance to stop him, to evade, to say no. Chris waited, all but holding his breath, watching like a hawk for any nuance of evasion or rejection. He felt electric with his need, with the desire to touch, caress, hold. In increments, the gap vanished until he hovered over Jamie's lips. They trembled, though Chris didn't sense any fear. Didn't see it in his eyes. There was only the way he tilted his chin a bare fraction to make the meeting happen.

Chris closed the last gap, the miniscule space between them where they didn't touch, yet he still felt the warmth of breath on his own skin. Braced above Jamie, Chris bowed to blanket Jamie's length, pinned between him and the wall. Jamie's lashes fluttered and fell, the surrender so sweet, Chris's heart flipped in his chest.

Chris's free hand raised and cupped over Jamie's ear, teasing the curls of hair within his reach. The hard brush of Jamie's cast snuck around Chris's waist. The weight settled, and the grip of fingers registered on the fabric of his shirt. Chris sighed when Jamie's other hand glided up his chest to settle on Chris's shoulder, a light firebrand of heat in his palm.

He danced the tip of his tongue in languid teases from corner to corner, enjoying the journey. Jamie's body trembled like a tossed leaf against him. He whimpered beneath Chris, reaching for more. Chris's control was wire-thin, but it was there unlike the kiss in his office, when he'd been surprised and unable to leash the wanting he'd been fighting for so long. The plundering of this kiss was gentle, the discoveries drowning him in sensation. Every touch, every breath.

Jamie's questing hand rose from his shoulder, gliding over his neck upward to clutch into Chris's hair. The seductive move shot shivers in erotic pulses down his spine. Chris ached to get closer. His wolf was all for that plan. It wasn't going to happen.

He'd deal with the repercussions of disappointing his wolf later, of that he was sure.

Withdrawing from the kiss, he studied Jamie's flushed face. The man had the face of an angel. Even if his wolf hadn't told him to pay attention, he would have been drawn to Jamie. He knew it without a doubt. He was gentle, a soft talker to the animals, and simply too gorgeous to not be attracted to him.

Pressed against Chris's chest, after a couple weeks of good food and far less stress than he'd been getting at home, Jamie was looking healthier, glowing as vitality returned to his lean frame.

Chris shifted his hand, stroking a thumb against a high cheekbone. "Sexy," he said, simply admiring. All the marks on Jamie's face had finally faded, his lip healed. The gorgeous man before him had been hidden by the damage his father had caused. Ed had been right. He was beautiful. Incredible. *Mine.*

He wanted to take that step so badly, Chris clawed the wall with his braced hand to control the urge. The flex of Jamie's fingers on his nape caused tingles beneath flesh as Jamie responded in kind.

Jamie's luminous gaze flicked up, then was hidden by lashes. "You're sexy," he replied. He surprised Chris when he tipped forward to rest on Chris's sternum, nuzzling into Chris's chest. He moaned in blissful pleasure. A slow sigh and a release of tension molded Jamie to Chris's body like a second skin.

Chris didn't know how long they stood like that, wrapped around one another. Time didn't matter. Right then, everything was perfect.

* * * *

Jamie was roused Sunday morning by a knock on his door. "Jamie? You awake yet?"

"Am now," he mumbled, digging into his pillow.

"I need to go to the clinic. There's been another fire."

That snapped Jamie fully awake. He raked a hand through his hair. He also realized there was more in Chris's voice. He hopped from the bed and wrenched open the door, his body not quite up to speed as he leaned on it. "What happened?"

There was a wash of anger over Chris's features. "The storage shed."

"Shit," Jamie hissed. "Give me five minutes."

Chris nodded and spun on a stiff leg, leaving him to dress and clean up. The clinic was packed with vehicles when they arrived. A fire truck, two police cruisers, and both Cade and Quade were there. Chris and Jamie joined the twins on the sidelines.

"Any more details?" Chris asked.

Jamie watched the three brothers.

"This is really starting to piss me off." Cade snarled, shaking his head to Chris's query. Jamie stayed near Chris's side, at his shoulder. He knew

Cade wouldn't hurt him, but it was ingrained to stay out of reach when faced with anyone's rage.

All they could do was stand and watch as the fire was eventually drowned in high-powered arcs of water.

Jamie watched as the three firefighters who'd worked the water began beating at the shed, advancing their paces with the water.

"All the feed," Quade said with a sigh.

Jamie crossed his arms over his stomach. The feed, extra supplies, equipment, braces. He couldn't imagine the loss they'd just suffered.

One of the uniformed officers approached and began questioning Quade. Cade came to stand beside Chris.

"At least it wasn't the main building," Chris muttered, a low burning fury thickening his voice.

"We'd be ruined," Cade stated, slanting his brother a look.

Jamie was thankful the donkeys had already been picked up by their owner. There hadn't been anything in the pens to injure.

Not too much later, the firemen backed out of the shed, stopping the rush of water. They began to clean up. One of them withdrew his safety helmet and beneath soaked hair stood Ed. He seemed surprised to spot Jamie but gave him a tight-lipped smile before resuming working around the rig.

While Quade was answering questions, another car maneuvered into the rear lot and stopped. A portly older man rolled from his car and joined them.

"Dr. Rose?"

All three brothers turned, but with Quade answering questions, the newcomer focused on him. Jamie spotted the badge dangling around his neck.

"Who is that?" he asked, leaning close to Chris.

"Probably the arson investigator."

Jamie bit on his lip. That made sense, but it also proved that this was bad. They remained at the clinic well into the morning answering questions and giving statements. Even Jamie, though Chris was never far from his side as he answered.

"I don't know about you guys, but I could use a coffee," Cade groused, leaning against one of the many cars, glaring at the now destroyed building. "Not what I meant when I said I wanted more excitement in my life."

Chris sighed. "I know. I really wanted to sleep in."

Jamie had too. The sun hadn't even peeked over the horizon when Chris had first knocked on his door that morning. Commiserating, he leaned and rubbed his temple to Chris's shoulder. Glancing down, Chris automatically draped an arm around his waist. "Let's go to Mabel's."

No one argued Chris's suggestion.

He squeezed Jamie. "Wait here."

Jamie nodded, watching as Chris approached the investigator. Cards were exchanged along with handshakes. He gave the building one last frowning look, then walked back. "Let's go."

Jamie clambered into the truck while Cade leaped the bed to sit in back, which left Quade to ride in the cab with them. This arrangement tucked Jamie up against Chris's side. He wasn't going to argue; it just took him by surprise. Chris gave him a soft smile, giving Jamie a fuzzy feeling inside.

Once at Mabel's the boys did the same thing: the twins together on one side of a broad booth leaving Chris and Jamie together with Jamie along the wall. Not pinned, but definitely encircled. Watching through his lashes, Jamie realized they didn't even know they were doing it. They were protecting him. No questions asked.

He wondered what it all meant.

"Hi, guys. Here early for a Sunday, aren't you?"

"Morning, Sissy," Cade said, greeting their waitress. "Problems gave us an early start. Coffee all the way."

"You bet. And for Jamie too?"

Jamie gaped, his eyes pinned on her rounded face. "You know my name?"

She laughed easily. "Honey, everyone in town knew your name two minutes after you were here. This isn't New York."

"Get him a large orange juice. He's still recovering." Chris slid a hand beneath the table and touched his thigh lightly.

Sissy winked and scurried away to get their orders.

"Chris," Jamie said, moaning with mild exasperation. He wasn't twelve.

"Jamie," he replied, copying him. "Trust me, a couple more days of orange juice won't kill you."

Jamie saw Cade and Quade both duck their heads, evading to hide their snickers. He gave Chris a light elbow in the ribs, which he dramatically *oomphed* over. That brought the laughter out all around.

"He's going to keep you on your toes," Cade said.

Chris didn't seem at all worried about that possibility. A few minutes later coffee and a tumbler of OJ were delivered to the table. They gave orders and were left alone again.

"So, any ideas on this morning?" Quade asked.

Chris cupped his mug, stirring in sugar and cream. "I didn't get close enough to know for sure, but I think the lock on the door was gone."

"But I know it was locked!" Jamie almost cried, horrified he could have screwed up. "I know I wouldn't have left it open."

"Jamie, I'm not blaming you." Chris touched his thigh again and this time left his hand there. "You are too careful to have left it open." Chris hung his head low to gaze upward though his lashes. "I think someone has a copy of the key."

"Why do you think that?" Cade asked, mulling over his own coffee.

"I didn't remember it until this happened, but about a month ago Lyla's keys went missing. For two days. Then she found them in the shed. That's why she wears them around her neck now."

Quade rubbed his chin. "That's right. I remember you asking us if we'd seen them."

Cade's expression grew thoughtful and then he nodded. "I do too."

Just then, Chris's cell phone rang. "This is Chris. No, not that I've ever known about. It would have been repaired if we'd seen it. Right. I understand. Let us know what you find out and when we can start cataloguing what we need to replace. Thank you." No one else at the table spoke until he was done.

He silenced the phone. His expression was even grimmer. "That was Detective Gentry. It seems someone has been using our shed for hiding drugs."

"Holy fuck," Cade muttered. "How'd we miss that?"

"A torn-up baseboard that we didn't cause," he answered. "He found a beat-up gym bag and other items that looked like they'd been there for a while." Chris looked at his brothers in turn as he continued. "He also found what started the fire. Someone had set up a small propane burner behind the shed, hidden from sight. There's no telling what was going on but it looks like someone had been using it and when it got out of hand, ran."

"Great." Quade rubbed the heels of his hands into his eyes. "Something that had been going on often?"

"He seemed to think so. He'll give us a more detailed report when he can."

Unable to bear the anger and worry this was causing all of them, Jamie reached below the table and curled Chris's hand into his. Chris twisted on his neck to meet Jamie's gaze.

"Thanks." He pressed a light kiss to Jamie's lips, which made him blush with a surge of heat he knew was visible under his skin. He jerked away, creating a gap. Searching the restaurant, it didn't look like anyone had paid them any attention.

"Don't worry. We're an open community," he told Jamie softly.

"Can I just stay here?" he asked, half-joking. He'd never expected it, but Silo was definitely looking better and better. A place to live, a job, friends, and gay-friendly. Better than anything he'd ever known.

"Thought you already were," Cade mentioned. He sat back from the table as plates arrived and slid into place before them.

Catching Chris's expression, Jamie was thinking Cade might be right.

## Chapter Thirteen

Chris dropped off Quade and Cade at the clinic to get their own vehicles after their late breakfast. The shed was roped off with yellow tape, but aside from that it was quiet and everyone had left. He hoped there were no more hassles over this. Whatever was going on had to stop. He added a prayer that it wasn't tied to anyone at the clinic.

He noticed that Jamie didn't scoot across the seat now that it was empty on his other side. The fact that Jamie liked being near him shot a bolt of energy through Chris's system.

He slid his arm behind Jamie's shoulders and tugged him into his chest. "This okay?" he asked gently.

Jamie snuggled in close with a quiet sigh. Chris took that for all the answer he was going to get or need. He was taking things a step at a time with Jamie. Cautiously. Jamie was growing comfortable. Chris definitely wasn't going to complain. He needed to earn his trust and give him a chance to understand before things got too far or moved too quickly.

Jamie slid out of the truck off the seat behind him when they reached the house. "I think I'm going to take a nap," Jamie said, stretching his arms over his head. "Is there anything you need done?"

"Nope. I'll check on Bear and Biscuit, then I'll be in."

"Okay."

Jamie dug the house key from a pocket and opened the door, letting himself in with Chris watching until he was gone. Walking around the house afterward, Chris studied the area. It didn't look like anything was amiss here. He whistled, and a few seconds later the earth-booming thunder of hooves could be heard.

"Hey, boys," he crooned, giving scratches between ears and eyes when they crowded up to the fence. "Behaving?" They just stood there, wallowing in the attention. He took several minutes, allowing Jamie time to settle in his room. The thought of him naked was giving Chris chills. It was a battle of restraint and control to not do more than he had with the younger man. The memory of their few shared kisses, touching him, when all he wanted to do was lean into his body and take in the scent that clung to his skin, wound through him. Or to run his tongue beneath Jamie's ear to capture the sweetness there. Crawl into him and stay there. He longed for the freedom to do those things and so much more with him.

Chris sighed, closing his eyes to lean against Tiberius's larger block of a head. "He's driving me nuts, Bear."

Maybe he should go for a run. He shouldn't be needed. Glancing over his shoulder, he debated for a moment. Jamie should be curled up in his room resting. There wasn't a risk. He was at home. And it was Sunday. Technically a free day for him.

Releasing Tiberius's halter he turned for the barn, slipping in through a side door. He stripped by one of the stalls. With the large bay doors open to the pastures, it was bright within. Getting down to skin was natural. It just felt odd because he knew he wasn't alone. Fear of discovery made him twitchy and rushed. He wanted to tell Jamie. It was too soon. He wasn't scared to admit he was terrified of Jamie's reaction. He was terrified the truth would scare Jamie so bad, Chris would lose him.

Once he stood bare as the day he was born, he drew a breath and let it happen, feeling the way sunlight struck his body in stripes of heat to change as his skin became covered in fur. He shook himself when he stood on four feet and studied the barn in silent appraisal, ensuring things were still quiet.

He padded to the pasture door and woofed, more of a whine really, to get Tiberius and Biscuit's attentions. They swung around and stamped their feet, shaking their heads. They weren't frightened by him and were comfortable, but just the same he wouldn't just hop out and cause panic. Chris warned them before he tore off into the land behind everything, hoping a long, hard run would help clear his mind and soothe his impatience.

There was little hope it would do anything about the need burning in his blood.

* * * *

Jamie burrowed into the pillow, slowly coming out of the haze of his whirling dreams. He couldn't remember anything about them, but he knew they hadn't been happy ones. Probably an overshadow

116

caused by this morning's fire mingling with his past. Regardless, he was happier he couldn't remember them.

Dragging out of bed, he aimed for the kitchen and water. A few deep guzzles, and he felt his brain getting back into the game. He glanced at the clock on the stove. He looked around, noticing that the house was silent. He'd been asleep for over an hour. Chris had to be around somewhere.

Jamie set the glass in the sink, then wandered the house but found quickly that it was empty.

"Huh." Well, Chris had said he'd check on the horses; maybe he was still out there doing stuff in the barn. He could have been in and out half a dozen times and Jamie wouldn't have known anything.

Opening the fridge, he dug through the bottom drawer and found the carrots, palming several. Tiberius was a pig when it came to carrots. Biscuit, for his bad reputation, was a delicate eater, light on skin, and not pushy. Jamie had discovered early on which of the two was the real menace when it came to snacks.

With the barn on the right and the pasture on the left, it was easy to find the horses. Only they weren't alone. Jamie's steps faltered as he became mesmerized in their antics. He tilted his head between his shoulders trying to figure out if he needed to go call someone for help or if they were just playing.

He did know this much: Jamie had no idea Tiberius could move like that. He swayed and twirled on his hind legs, mindful of the large dog that was darting around his feet. It looked like a dog, a big, shaggy, nearly black something. There wasn't any real barking or growling. He swore it looked like they were playing tag. The dog would get right up to Tiberius's nose and then backflip to run, with Tiberius nipping at a tail that waved like a flag, taunting the large horse.

Except in all the time he'd been living at Chris's, he'd never once seen any dog. Jamie was trying to figure out whether or not it was dangerous when a vehicle pulled around the house. A yellow Jeep.

Shading his eyes, he realized it was Ed. Searching the pasture once more, the dog had vanished. It must have been startled by the Jeep pulling in.

"Hey," Ed called, landing on his feet when the vehicle stilled. "Jamie, right?" He walked up but didn't crowd him. "You're looking better."

"Thanks." Jamie took a step toward the fence, aware he still clutched the carrots. He made noises to get the horses' attentions.

"I saw you this morning at the fire." Like Ed was surprised he would have been there.

Jamie met his eyes, then swept away. "Thanks for what you did."

Ed shrugged, standing beside Jamie at the fence but not too close. "Where's Chris?"

"I think in the barn," he said. It was the next logical guess. He wasn't inside, and he wasn't about to tell Ed he didn't know. He might be friends with Chris, but Jamie didn't trust him.

Jamie stroked flat faces, then handed over the treats. The horses munched in contented silence.

"I heard you're working at the clinic now."

Jamie hiked a shoulder. Small-town gossip really did move at the speed of sound. Not that anyone was hiding it, but after Mabel confirmed that everyone knew who he was that morning, he wasn't at all surprised that anyone else knew he worked for his current landlord-slash-roommate.

Ed moved a little closer. "You like it?"

"So far."

"Are you staying?"

Ed was getting closer, his voice dropping. Trying to draw Jamie out. It wasn't going to work. The man was huge and obviously used his size to his advantage if he worked with the fire department. His closeness was making the skin under Jamie's pits damp.

"I haven't decided yet," he hedged, feeling conflicted after that morning's revelations. He wanted to stay, but he didn't want Ed to know that. Frankly, Jamie didn't feel it was any of his business.

"Would you like to go out, catch a movie? I want to get to know you better." He was cajoling, using a sweet-as-honey tone.

"Uh…" Jamie's mouth dried up. He kept feeding the horses chunks of carrot to seem occupied. Not like he was giving it any real thought. There was no way he'd go anywhere secluded with this man.

"Hey, Ed."

Both Ed and Jamie swung around. Chris walked out of the barn wiping his hands on a towel, brown stains prevalent.

"Hey. Came by to see how you guys were after this morning." Ed was going for nonchalant and neighborly concerned. Jamie wasn't buying it, not after he just hit on Jamie.

Chris gave Jamie a quick once-over and even though it felt possessive, he didn't hate it like the way he was reacting to Ed oozing closer.

"Waiting for the final arson report. It'll be a mess, but it's replaceable."

Chris tucked the stained rag into a rear pocket. There was a faint smell now, something like musk and oil. He must have been working in the barn and heard Ed pull in. It was almost a relief really to know he wasn't all alone.

"That's good." Ed fell silent, crossing his arms to lean against the fence planks. "Given any more thought to last time?"

Chris scowled. "No, and the answer is still no."

"Fine." Ed pushed from the fence. "I'll talk to you later." He managed to catch Jamie's eye. "You too," he offered to Jamie. Though kinder and more sensual, it still felt hollow.

Once he'd pulled out and left them in a cloud of hazy dust, Jamie rolled his eyes.

"He was hitting on you, wasn't he?"

Jamie faced the horses and hid his frown. Was he going to accuse Jamie of something? It wasn't like he had been encouraging Ed.

"Hey," Chris soothed him, coming up behind him. A light hand on Jamie's shoulder felt good, comforting. "If he ever gets pushy, tell him no, and if that doesn't work, call me."

"He doesn't seem picky," Jamie interjected.

"There's not a lot to choose from here." Chris's touch lingered on his shoulder, drifting until the weight was gone.

"Is that why you're being so nice to me?"

Chris took the spot Ed had been standing in. "No, but I won't lie to you. I am attracted to you."

Jamie digested that. "What does that mean?"

"It means I like being with you, like kissing you, definitely like touching you."

Jamie's lashes lowered a few increments. He liked all of that too. He wasn't ashamed to admit he hoped there was more of it.

The light stroke of the back of Chris's fingers floated over his cheek.

"You're amazing, Jamie," he said.

Tiberius mouthed at Jamie's hand, hunting for more carrots. He petted him in answer since he was out.

"I want you to be happy here first. That is more important than anything else."

"I just don't understand why," Jamie said, not looking away from the soft velvet of Tiberius's lips rubbing over the top of his hand. Looking into Chris's eyes right now would be too much, total overload, and he'd crumple at this man's feet.

Chris turned and faced the horses. "You keep saying that I'm doing all of this because I want something. You're right."

Jamie was afraid to breathe. *Here it comes.*

"I want you to be happy. I want you to be able to feel secure enough to smile. You have the sweetest smile," Chris said, then pressed his lips together as though he'd said too much.

"You think so?" Jamie asked. He hadn't expected any of that.

Jamie's heart tripped when Chris directed his chin toward him with a light touch. Jamie clutched at the top rail of the fence when his knees shook.

"When you smile for me... I can't explain it." The slight exploratory stroke of Chris's thumb against his bottom lip shot desire through his body in a wave. It filled his veins. "You're beautiful, Jamie. An amazing kind of man. I can't stop the way I want you, so there's no point in lying about it."

"Oh God." He shivered under the hot sun. "Chris." The sound of Chris's name on Jamie's tongue was no less than a growl.

## Chapter Fourteen

The kiss was unexpected for both of them. Chris hadn't intended to go this far, but it was beginning to feel so natural it was worse than difficult to ignore those lips. He *wanted* to kiss Jamie. Thankfully Jamie wanted him too, as he tipped in answer and circled Chris's neck with his arms, drawing them together.

Chris looped his arms around Jamie and hugged him close, savoring as well as drowning in the younger man's heat. Jamie whimpered, that same throaty sound he'd made before when Chris had captured him against the wall at the clinic. It drove him out of his mind. Chris moaned. Jamie was like spun sugar and twice as sweet, delicate-looking yet there was more to him than met the eye. A backbone of steel. All of Jamie called to Chris like a wicked temptation.

Gliding from his lips, Chris panted, trying to catch his breath. "I have to make a small change."

"Hmm," Jamie murmured drowsily. His head rolled loosely on his neck as Chris investigated, roaming over skin and pulse points with his mouth.

"I *definitely* love kissing you."

Jamie's head sank forward and burrowed into him. Chris felt Jamie rocking his forehead on Chris's shoulder, likely in denial. Chris knew those kisses would be his downfall for the rest of his life, and he was perfectly okay with that. Fingers danced into the length of his hair, teasing at Chris's nerves with flicks of need.

He nibbled on a soft earlobe, soaking up the shiver that flew down Jamie's frame. Tucking Jamie just a hair closer, Chris brought their pelvises together, rocking them.

Jamie gasped, drawing to a moan. The demanding pulse of flesh captured between them surged against Chris's body. Needing.

"Jamie." He nipped at the soft spot beneath the earlobe he'd just tortured. Chris wanted to roam, lick, and devour every square inch of this man's body. Holding him steady, he palmed the tight rounds of his ass and hesitated, waiting for resistance or rejection. Jamie only wiggled closer. Hefting his lighter frame against his chest, Chris carried him to the other side of the barn where the grass was thickest. Jamie hooked his legs around Chris's waist, clinging to him. The press of his cock in his jeans was killing Chris where Jamie rubbed into his abdomen with each stride. He couldn't stop sucking and nibbling on Jamie's neck.

A moment later he knelt carefully, gliding Jamie to stretch out in the soft grass. "You look incredible right there, like this."

Jamie watched him with cautious, bright eyes. Chris didn't blame him for the doubts.

"Never hurt you, Jamie," he said, hanging over him on flat palms.

"I think I believe you." He tilted his chin, not losing Chris's gaze. Wariness? Yes. Fear? No.

Jamie was quite a few inches shorter than Chris, and lying together their lengths were perfect when he shifted to rest by Jamie's side. Chris nuzzled close, amazed when Jamie's eyes fluttered and a slow, languid sigh slipped from him. He trusted Chris more than he realized. The realization soared within Chris.

Jamie followed when Chris urged him into a kiss. It was slow and easy, unlike the unfettered passion of the day before. Teasing and languid, a kiss that could take all day. When Jamie raised to a shoulder, then to an elbow to roll Chris to his own back, he went without a fight.

He watched silently as Jamie investigated and kissed, little kitten licks of his tongue that drove Chris insane with wanting. Insects buzzed nearby, and the sounds of nature were a distant hum in his ears. His entire focus was Jamie.

Chris raised a hand to thread into tousled hair. Jamie tipped into the caresses. "Feels good," Jamie said with a sigh. He glided to sling a leg between Chris's, rubbing seductively against Chris's thigh. He didn't say much, but the proof of how much he liked the pressure was in the shivers that skated down his frame in freefall.

With the hand teased through Jamie's dark gold hair, Chris brought him down for a kiss. Light tugs pulled the hem of Chris's shirt out of his jeans waist. The shock of fingertips on sun-heated skin was electric, and he groaned. The soft curl of lips against Chris's was unmistakable.

Propped on a bent elbow, Jamie slithered his free hand beneath Chris's shirt, fingers splayed in seductive discovery. Chris writhed, trying to get more of that taunting hand. The longer Jamie explored, the more confident he grew until finally he paused over the sensitive skin of Chris's nipple. Chris sucked on Jamie's lip, going crazy under his curious touch.

"Can I see?" Jamie's whispered words were as sweet as the breeze against Chris's flushed skin.

Nudging him away, Chris crunched upward, yanking his shirt off with impatient tugs. He loved Jamie's curiosity. He'd always taken the lead, knowing what he wanted from his bed partners. Now with his wolf involved, both he and his spirit could lie there and bask in Jamie's learning touch. He arched his throat in surrender as Jamie sucked and licked from his jaw downward. Quiet moans of pleasure kept his blood racing, his dick stiff and pinned. He refused to scare Jamie, so giving it any attention was out of the question.

"Ahhh." Chris moaned when Jamie swiped his tongue over his chest. He panted. *Evil.*

"Chris?"

"Never hurt you, baby. Anything you want to do." He followed Jamie's progress through slit eyelids. He cushioned his head on a crooked forearm in the thick grass, his fingers still lightly embedded and flexing behind Jamie's head, encouraging. "All yours, if you want it."

Jamie raised his head, sweet blue eyes piercing him. He felt staked to the ground. Couldn't move.

"Hard to stay away from you," Jamie murmured to return to the flat valley of his sternum.

A fresh wave of hunger and need swamped Chris, tightening skin. He all but melted beneath Jamie's lips. The next few minutes completely swept his brain clear, his inhibitions and control out the window. Nipping teeth, damp tongue, and caring lips. Jamie was *adoring* him. Because he was so deep in the bliss, it took a few seconds to register the change in pressure around his waist.

First the button, then the slow bite of teeth as the zipper nudged down. He trembled when Jamie buried his nose in the opened gap of his jeans. Jamie burrowed his nose into the V of Chris's legs and unable to not move, he widened his straddle invitingly. Jamie hungrily dived, working his jeans out of the way to suck and lick at the crease of Chris's hip.

"Shit," Chris hissed. Whatever Jamie wanted, it was his. *Anything.*

He arched his back, and his jeans and briefs were tugged down enough to let his cock pop free. Chris moaned in relief, his vision filled with azure blue sky. Blood pulsed, making him rigid and sensitive. Every little tease of breeze sent chills up his spine. Sunlight warmed him, and Jamie's touch set him on fire.

Jamie's long fingers wrapped around his pulsing length, holding him at the base to stroke him once. Chris cried out as Jamie closed incredible lips around the crown, sipping to ride him with a flourish to the tip. Jamie's moan of pleasure was music.

Then it was like he hit a new gear, engulfing as much of Chris's length as he could. The hard press of Jamie's tongue was heaven and hell in a single touch. Jamie shifted to a better position, then there was no hesitation as he swallowed and bobbed, riding him with a mouth that was nothing less than sin.

"Jamie." Chris was quickly racing to the edge of his climax. Jamie purred in encouragement. Tingles shot in every direction from the vibration. "Baby," Chris whined. "Com—" Chris gasped, his spine arching as Jamie tickled at his perineum. He clutched reflexively at the back of Jamie's head, the first shocking blast slicing through his body to be followed by several more.

Jamie sucked and swallowed until Chris was spent.

Panting, he laid in the grass with his eyes closed. Licked and cared for until he was clean. Jamie released his still-pulsing dick as he went soft. He rested on a cheek to Chris's stomach, his breath hot and short. Chris petted his hair, the thick strands a little damp from his efforts.

"Come here." He tugged lightly, and drowsy eyes opened to snag on his. He found Jamie's lips for a sweet kiss. He danced against Jamie's tongue, moaning at the bitter hint of semen he found. "You are one in a million."

Jamie's lashes lowered, a flush of heat tinting his cheeks.

Once Chris felt he had the strength to make his body obey him, he urged Jamie across his chest, his arms banding Jamie's smaller body with gentle strength. He felt Jamie's need pressing into his hip. Chris slid his fingertips into thick hair at Jamie's temple, easing it up and back. "Can I take care of that for you, sweetheart?"

Jamie's breath whooshed from him in a rush. "You want to?"

"In so many ways," he replied, hiding the growl of hunger by biting at Jamie's shoulder. *Suck you, lick you, stroke you, love you.* The list was endless for Chris.

"They usually didn't..." Jamie drifted off, avoiding looking upward to Chris again.

"Ah, baby. They didn't bother, or didn't offer?"

"Neither," came the whisper of sound.

Chris hugged him tighter. "Jamie." He tucked Jamie into his chest, nuzzling, wanting him to know he was so completely wanted. He toed off his sneakers and worked his jeans down and off, leaving him naked in the shade of the barn. He doubted Jamie would allow him to see every inch, but he was determined to worship what Jamie gave him.

He wiggled Jamie to lay flat on top of his chest. Stroking his hair, back, and shoulders, anywhere he could reach while he gazed into the bluest of eyes. Jamie nestled into the wider splay of his legs. Featherlight strokes of fingers danced from Jamie's temple down his neck, resting on his pulse. He rubbed circles with his thumbs above Jamie's collarbones. Not hiding his intent, he undid the first button of Jamie's shirt. The top two were open at his throat. That sexy dip in skin called for the swirl of Chris's tongue.

Chris arched his head and found it, humming as he drank in Jamie's taste and scent, licking that perfect hollow. Jamie shivered above him, resting on bent arms. The angle brought his head nearly temple-to-temple with Chris. Then Chris was inching his fingers between their chests to undo the next button. The pulse of Jamie's heart was clear beneath his skin.

Jamie could escape like a darting sparrow, if he chose. Chris touched him, but didn't restrain him. As the next button came undone, Jamie's breathing hitched, yet he remained perfectly still.

Gliding a hand beneath fabric, Chris touched his chest. Firm, smooth skin. The slope of his body dipping to his waist. Sweeping up in languid strokes, he found the silken, taut skin of his bud. Jamie shivered even beneath the heat of the day, though he didn't try to run.

He undid one more button and then stopped. "It's up to you if there's more." The way they lay together blocked Chris's inquisitive investigation of Jamie's body.

Slowly, Jamie rose and stared with unblinking eyes at Chris. The flesh of his neck danced with the erratic tempo of his heart. Without ever losing that connection he slid off Chris's chest, relinquishing the safety of escape to rest on his spine next to him.

Chris caressed the side of his face, his heart in his throat as he absorbed the gift Jamie had just given him, knowing what he'd faced, and the lack of love in his life. Lowering, he gently kissed him. And knew without a doubt that he was falling for the other man. Falling hard.

## Chapter Fifteen

Jamie couldn't tear himself away from the gentle caresses. No one had ever touched him with such care. It made breathing hard as his lungs hitched and his heart fluttered. Not out of nervousness, but out of need. Wanting more, but scared to ask for it.

It didn't seem to matter. Chris seemed to know, and was serious about giving him whatever he wanted, even without saying a word about what he craved.

He pulled the remainder of Jamie's shirt out of his jeans and undid the last two buttons, spreading it to expose Jamie's chest. The worst of the bruises were gone, though the spot over his ribs was still tender. As if he knew, Chris lowered and licked and kissed where he hurt with a touch lighter than a butterfly. Jamie clenched his hand, grabbing grass in his fist in reaction. He trembled so hard, it's a wonder the barn didn't rattle next to them.

"Shh." Chris chuckled. He rubbed his nose into Jamie's stomach, tickling him along the way.

"No… It's good," Jamie rasped. His chest was jumping with harsh pants. *Please don't stop!*

Chris resumed his languorous attack on Jamie's body. Jamie was floating higher than the sky above them. There weren't any clouds today, so the sky was limitless. The firm stroke of a hot tongue rolled over his ribs, up his sternum, across his collarbone. Like he couldn't get enough.

Then Chris encircled the small pink flesh of his nipple and flicked it with a devilish tongue. Jamie arched, gasping as sparks lit from his nape downward.

"Mmm," Chris hummed, not letting up in the least as he tasted every inch of viewable skin.

God, Jamie had never felt this! He was sure he was going to go up in a burst of desire. He rolled his hips, aching in unbelievable need.

"Can I?"

Chris was sipping soft kisses to his abdomen, nudging against the edge of his jeans waist.

"Yes!" He wanted to shout it, but it was more of a plea. Jamie was glad he was able to say anything at all as hard as he was gulping air to feed desperate lungs.

Chris's soothing touch was on him again, petting in circles to then stroke down his ribs.

"You're beautiful, Jamie. Absolutely incredible."

Jamie couldn't argue without any air in his lungs, but it didn't stop the *you're nuts* from popping into his mind.

As though Chris had heard it, he smothered a soft laugh into Jamie's stomach. Then everything from the sound of the breeze in the trees to the occasional noise from the horses on the other side vanished.

Chris had bared his groin. Shivers tracked up and down his frame. "Chris."

"I got you, baby."

Jamie's heart pounded like a mallet into a drum skin in the scant seconds before the first brush of warm breath, before the first flick of wet contact.

Jamie's loose hand clutched at Chris's shoulder, hot skin from desire and sunlight. He'd held his cast-covered arm at his side, unmoving, though he couldn't stop the flex and clutch of his fingers in the grass.

Then Chris was slowly gliding over Jamie's shaft. Pressure became cataclysmic pleasure as Chris took more and more. Jamie gasped and moaned. His eyelids closed, drowning in the heat, tossed into a whirlpool of feeling. Chris swirled and played, nipped and sucked.

Jamie whined and whimpered. He couldn't stop, hiking his hips, seeking and getting what he needed. It was beyond anything he'd ever received. There was a light wiggle on his jeans, not much, just enough to slip them below his balls. He quickly found out why.

He cried out, almost sobbing as Chris loved on tight skin. A lapping tongue had him growling and panting, unbelievable kisses that were hotter than a flame to nerves.

"Love the way you smell, Jamie. Raw and sweet."

Jamie heard him. He had no clue what he was talking about. He didn't really care just so long as he didn't stop. Chris's touch was hotter than lightning, points of need so strong he was lost beneath his talented lips.

"Okay, baby. This is for you."

Jamie blinked, gasping and panting. Then Chris took his full length, taking him deep and rolling against every sensitive inch with the hard press of his tongue.

"Chris!"

He played with Jamie's sac, then stole his sanity when he rimmed Jamie's hole with a light finger.

*"Ahhhhh! Chris!"* He couldn't stop the orgasm. It was like he wasn't even in his own body the way his climax ripped through him. It sliced him in two. Chris moaned, devouring every jet and drop. It was so fast, he felt like an untried virgin. He'd been touched, sucked, whatever, but this... He buried his face in a bent arm, embarrassed at his lack of control. He wanted to crawl away, but felt too boneless to move a muscle.

Rasped breath burned his throat as his humiliation deepened.

"Shh." Chris had crawled up his length and folded him into his chest. "It's okay." He stroked Jamie's back, bare chest to bare chest.

Jamie hid himself in Chris's shoulder and neck, just trying to breathe without breaking down into tears. Something he'd *never* done, not even when his father had almost killed him.

"Was it bad?" Chris asked, subdued and clearly serious.

"No!" Jamie jerked in his arms to stare into Chris's face, appalled that he'd even *think* that. "Me... I..." He clenched his eyes shut, unable to meet Chris's understanding. He bit his lip, trying to gather words. "You must think I'm pathetic. No control." He slumped.

Chris tucked him into his shoulder. He crooned soothingly. "Never, Jamie. I'd like to think I drove you nuts and you lost it."

"You did," he replied, the softest two words of his life. "It was impossible *not to.*"

Chris murmured more tender words. "Then there is absolutely nothing you did wrong. It was incredible, Jamie. You, wild under my touch, moaning like a sexy animal." He nuzzled at Jamie's temple. "I loved every minute of it. Every single second. And you taste addictive." Slowly Jamie began to relax, the constant sweep of a strong hand nonstop on his back. "I'm the lucky one right now," Chris whispered against his ear.

"How?" Jamie still felt like an inexperienced teenager, not nearly mollified by Chris's show of patience.

"I have you, I'm holding you, and I'm not letting you go," he explained. He lifted Jamie's chin with a curved finger. "I've waited weeks to see if you felt this."

Jamie swallowed. "This?" A rush of heat? A need to touch? He couldn't begin to explain it, just praying that Chris understood. By the solemn calm on his face, he did.

Chris nodded. "I *want* to have this, and more, with you. Only you." He settled a tender kiss on Jamie's mouth. Playfulness tipped sinful lips at the corners, hidden mirth making Chris's eyes sparkle in the sunlight. "If I happen to make you lose it once or twice, I think my ego can take it."

Jamie groaned and sank his head forward again to smack into Chris's shoulder with a dull thud. The action made Chris laugh with a low, throaty sound, pleased and content. Jamie circled him with clinging arms, sharing that feeling with him.

He realized the dark inadequacy he felt had been swept clean from his thoughts.

\* \* \* \*

"Okay, Jamie. Hold still."

Jamie followed Dr. Hoover's instructions and didn't dare twitch as he worked the saw over the cast. Dust spewed and inch by inch, he felt the rough release as plaster cracked. A few moments later, Dr. Hoover set the saw aside and grasped the cast. With a single snap, the cast split enough to work his arm free.

He sighed in relief as he wiggled his wrist and flexed his fingers.

"How does it feel?"

"Lighter," he remarked through a thankful smile.

Chris's comforting hand on a shoulder had him glancing upward. Tender humor was there for him.

"The X-ray looked good. It'll feel different for a few days as you limber the muscles again. However, if you have any swelling, heat, or pain, come see me immediately."

"I will, and thank you." He grinned for the doctor who gave him a pat on a knee, signaling that he was done.

"Better?" Chris asked.

"Much." Jamie unrolled the cuff of his shirt to button, something he hadn't been able to do with his left arm since the night the cast had been placed.

He leaned into Chris's strength when he curled an arm around Jamie, standing together. "Thank you," Jamie told him as they left Dr. Hoover's examination room.

"You're welcome, baby." Chris lowered and kissed him gently. Since the afternoon by the barn, Chris had been attentive, sweet, and not in the least bit demanding. They often snuggled on the couch to watch TV, but still slept in separate rooms. Jamie knew Chris was waiting for him to make that choice, letting him become comfortable in the new direction their friendship had rocketed off into before taking it to the next level.

Honestly, he wanted it, but it still terrified him. What would happen when he took that step and then Chris decided he'd played enough? It was a frightening tangent for Jamie, leaping into the unknown. There'd never been anyone special in his life, never been a serious lover who wanted him for more than a sneaked release. Jamie knew he couldn't be who he was around his dad, which was what had prompted the admission that night. He wanted his freedom.

It nearly cost him his life. He sighed, pushing the memories away. That had happened two months before, and he was nowhere near his father now.

They walked together on the sidewalk in front of the town business fronts. "Mabel's?" Chris asked.

"Pancakes?" *Jeez, but does he know me or what?* Chris knew his weakness for hotcakes and real butter.

"A double stack."

Jamie laughed lightly. He was nearly floating when he was with Chris like this. At work, they were a team, professional, with barely a spared heated glance if there was even time for it. Any other time was theirs.

Chris held the glass door to Mabel's open wide. Just as Jamie was about to walk through, lost on Chris's profile and smile, he was snagged quickly into Chris's chest. Focusing forward, he realized he'd almost walked right into Ed.

"Sorry!" Jamie gasped.

"Hey, Ed," Chris greeted evenly.

Ed took one look at the pair of them, his mouth thinning, then his shoulders sagged. "Never had a chance, did I?"

Jamie didn't know what to say, not meaning to hurt the other man. Jamie didn't want him, but that hadn't meant hurting him. Before Jamie could think of anything to say, Ed walked past them without looking back once to climb into his Jeep, a steaming cup of coffee in his hand.

"Come on, baby," Chris urged gently. A light hand cupped his waist, gliding to the dip of his spine, all at once possessive and protective. The Jeep was gone by the time they sat at a booth.

"Will he be all right?" Jamie asked, glancing out the window then to Chris, who sat at his shoulder. It made him warm inside that Chris sat beside him, rather than across from him. It made it easier to hold hands beneath the table.

"Yes. Silo just doesn't have what he needs."

Reading his expression, Jamie felt there was more in those words but didn't want to pry. A moment later, Sissy arrived with water and menus for them to order.

## Chapter Sixteen

Chris sat at the kitchen table, carefully reading over the report from Detective Gentry. Cade and Quade also had copies. Chris raised his head and drew a breath hunting to speak, then realized Jamie was at work. He blew it out harshly, frustrated that he wasn't there, couldn't talk to him, couldn't see him. Couldn't touch him. His wolf whined.

"Yeah, yeah," he griped. He flipped the page in his hand and set it face-down on the table to read the next part.

They had managed to lift a very few half and partial fingerprints, but because of the fire and then the fabric of the satchel they'd found beneath the floorboards, there hadn't been many. It was of no one on record. The only connection they did have was that it seemed the one undamaged needle that Jamie had spotted that first morning was a match to the items from the fire. It was miniscule, but it was proof and a connection, which likely also included the damaged pair and bag Jamie had managed to drag from the Dumpster.

The jingle tone of his cell phone interrupted his review of the report. "Hello?"

"Hi, Chris."

"What's up, Lyla?" His brow scrunched. She usually didn't call him on his off hours.

"Jamie's dad found him," she whispered.

"Is he there now?" Chris was halfway out of his chair before she spoke again.

"No. I don't want him to know I'm telling you. I don't trust him, Chris. He called here, and I know he threatened Jamie. He went outside for a few seconds."

"How did he find him?"

"Joyce put him on the staff page."

Chris rubbed a hand down his face, sinking down into his chair, ready to sink to the floor for putting Jamie in danger.

"Crap. The door. Thanks for calling! Bye!" she said with false cheer, then hung up on him. Chris cleared the screen and stared at the phone. Joyce only did what she did for everyone. No one had even thought of that being an issue. It wasn't like they broadcast their employees for Tony nominations. Which meant his father had been actively searching for him.

But why? Jamie wasn't going to be giving his father any more of his money. There was less than a negative chance for his father to hurt Jamie. All three of the brothers would protect him, just like Chris would protect any mate of the twins'. It came down to family, and Jamie was part of their family. At least he would be when Chris could win him over completely and finally admit the whole shebang and claim him, and then he would be part of the pack as well.

Another hot breath and a face rub followed that thought. There had to be a way to bring this up, to show Jamie so he could understand. So he wouldn't be terrified of Chris, in any form. He knew he'd seen him that day playing with Tiberius. Though

140

he hadn't mentioned it, likely thinking he was nothing more than a dog, so it wasn't important. He had to tell Jamie. He had to keep him safe. Chris had a strong feeling that they weren't done with Jamie's dad.

Lifting his phone, he dialed a number from memory. When it was answered, he only said, "I need to talk to you."

"Come over now."

"Yes, sir." Gathering the pages to slide into their folder, he left it on the table and strode to the rear door. He stripped, placing his things on the floor in a neat, folded pile, then cautiously opened the door. Ensuring that it was quiet and he was alone, he walked through the door to close it. Dropping forward, he was at a full run in seconds.

* * * *

Jamie's heart thudded erratically as he sagged to the back of the clinic wall. He covered his face with his hands and breathed. Or tried to.

Clive had found him. The fear he'd managed to push away swamped him in an avalanche of memories. Being the faceless body in a sea of nobodies in Silo hadn't been nearly unknown enough. Just what he'd feared. Not far enough. Not crowded enough. He shivered hard, feeling the rough exterior of the building dig into his shoulders.

Jamie could take his abuse, but he refused to have that man come to Silo and hurt someone he cared for, which he'd just discovered was a lot of people. Everyone he worked with. Cade and Quade.

And Chris. He swallowed the choked sob. He'd die if anything happened to Chris.

"You are mine, Jamie! My son, my flesh and blood. You *will* stop this rebellious bullshit." Jamie held the phone away from his ear, wincing at the roared yelling. Even four months ago he would have caved, right there. But not now.

When he was done, breathing heavily into the phone Jamie told him, "No, I'm not. It's your house, your bills. You pay them. You kicked me out, remember?" The anger he'd never given in to made his voice shake. "You kicked out your only son."

"You said you were gay!"

"I still am! You are not my father, and you never have been. You're a drunken leech. I do not know you," he finished icily, then hung up on him. He spun and dashed out the back door of the clinic, flopping to the wall where he now stood, his face buried in his hands. Shock at how he'd screamed at his dad, at work… *Shit.* He banged his head to the wall in recrimination. *At work,* no less.

He rolled his head forward to rub at the abused spot. Wiping his eyes with the heel of a hand, he thought he saw something out of the corner of his vision. He snapped straight. Clearing them with a quick swipe of his uniform top, he pushed off the building.

Yes, something or someone was moving behind the burned-out shed and the pens. They ducked down in the shadows, pawing through the grass. He heard their movements as they hunted, or whatever it was they were doing back there. Regardless, *they* weren't supposed to be there at all.

"Hey!" He pushed off the building. The person leaped upward, going ramrod straight before spinning and bursting into a full, wild run. "Hey! Stop!" He sprinted after the figure. They dashed past the pens and into the scrub behind the clinic. He could make out a lean guy, but not much more. He wore jeans and a dark T-shirt, but nothing that he could see to describe. He was fast, but Jamie hadn't been a track runner for nothing. They clawed through the grasses, legs swishing loudly as they pumped. He was gaining on him, with the other man cutting the path when the man he chased made a flying leap over something Jamie couldn't see.

Brittle ground vanished from under Jamie before he could skid to a stop. Roots struck him like sword edges, clawing at his legs and arms as he slid downward. Loose rock all but melted away beneath his feet, and there was nothing but air for a heartbeat or two. Loose dirt eclipsed him in an explosive cloud of dust as he fell. He rolled to the bottom finally, a hard landing. A whimpered moan leaked free before his world went black.

* * * *

When Chris arrived at the two-story cabin he paused at the property line, sniffing to ensure he was there alone and was welcome. As he approached the home, he spotted the fresh robe hanging on the hook beside the door. He left the shape of his four-footed spirit to gain two feet, then donned the robe. Once it was on and tied, he knocked to listen for the call. Given permission, he stepped through the doorway.

It had been more than a year since he'd been in his alpha's home. It wasn't luxurious, just the basic home of a man who'd been secure in his place in life and with his pack for many years. He was well respected in both forms. The image he portrayed outside of his home, in the courtroom, was the one that made the strongest impact, and it was one that he knew intimidated. Within these walls he was simply another man, a leader to those who needed him, but nothing more.

Chris walked to the den and stopped at the door, bowing his head to wait for admittance.

A large man in black slacks and a lightweight shirt, also black, turned from the bar near the fireplace. "You are welcome, son of Peter and Deena."

"Thank you, Alpha."

"What troubles you, Chris?"

Chris raised his eyes with the leave to do so. "I found the one I wish to make my mate." He accepted the small tumbler of liquor and sank to a nearby couch, Roman taking the empty wing chair in front of the cold fireplace. Chris took a tentative sip, searching for words to explain. He tugged on the robe to give his hands something to do. "I never got to talk to Dad about this."

Alpha nodded in understanding. "The young man?"

"Yes."

"Do you love him?"

Chris snapped his focus to Roman. Chris knew he cared deeply for Jamie, adored him, really. Was it love?

Roman waved an elegant hand. "If he is your true half, it will happen. You are tense. There's more."

Chris took a healthier drink of the bourbon, then licked his lips. "You probably know his story, about his father and why he left home."

Roman motioned that he did, a slight flick of his fingers. It didn't surprise Chris. Roman would know the movement of a fly in Silo if it affected his pack.

"His father found him today. He's not here, but I don't doubt he'll do something."

"So what is the problem? If and when he arrives, he'll be taken care of."

"I'm scared, Alpha," Chris choked out. Heat crawled up his face. He did *not* want to be having this conversation with his alpha. There was no other option. "He may run again."

Roman blinked, then tipped his head back and laughed deeply. Confused, Chris stifled the glare intended for his alpha. Unsure about his reaction, Chris waited, though he didn't understand what it was he'd said that made his alpha laugh like that. Wasn't sure he liked it, either.

After a moment, Roman leaned nearer with an elbow on a side of the chair. "Christopher, you are such your father's son. It's good to see it. You should be anxious, but not for that fear. If Jamie is your mate, as we each are blessed, he will fight the hardest by your side."

That was what he was afraid of. He didn't want to risk Jamie, not for anything. And definitely not against his own parent.

"How do I tell him?" Chris's gaze fell to the floor between them. That was his greatest fear. That he'd frighten Jamie so deeply, he'd lose him over the truth.

"You can tell him, but seeing is believing," Alpha advised gently. "The hardest thing I've ever known is the mating ritual for a nonshifter."

Chris winced, the liquor burning in his throat now. He hadn't allowed himself to think that far ahead. "He's already been through so much," he said, nearly inaudibly.

"Do you believe he trusts you?"

Chris didn't even think twice before he answered. "Yes."

"Then you're already at a place many won't find."

Those words brought Ed to mind, and he knew his alpha was right.

"Are you any closer to finding the vandals who burned your property?"

"No. I have the report and can claim it to the insurance." It was a reprieve considering, but it also told him that there wasn't much more he could pick out of Roman's brain. He handed his tumbler forward. "Thank you for your time, Alpha."

"You're welcome, Chris."

He bowed his head in deference, then turned on a heel to retrace the steps he'd made to get there. Now he had to get home. The run would give him time to think. He hoped somewhere along the way, he could also hatch a plan.

## Chapter Seventeen

Chris entered the clinic after closing time and, seeing the waiting room empty, locked the doors behind him. He walked to the offices and only found Cade.

"Busy day?"

Cade looked up. "Not too bad." He frowned. "What are you doing here?"

"Picking up Jamie." He did it every day. Why would today be different?

"But I thought he already left. I haven't seen him in a couple hours and thought he was already gone with you."

Chris went stock still. His dad couldn't be there already, could he? "You haven't seen him?"

Cade shook his head. "No. I know about the call he got and let him have some space."

Chris's heart tripped. *Where is he?* "His dad's not here, though, right?"

Cade grimaced. "Not that I know of. I wonder where he is." He stood from behind the desk. "I'm sure he's here."

Together they quickly checked the building, both turning up empty. "Did Lyla take him home with her?"

Chris shook his head. "He would have told me or just waited here."

Cade looked around him again, then nodded. "Yeah, he would have."

"Let me check his locker." Chris walked to the break room and peered through the mesh gate. "His wallet is still in there." His stomach was starting to knot up. Something was wrong.

"Okay. He's here somewhere, then."

Cade followed Chris out the rear door. Chills were coating Chris's arms. It was dead quiet out there. "Jamie!" Silence was his answer.

Chris pulled out his cell phone. Finding a number on his list, he hit dial, his heart in his throat. "Lyla?"

"Hi, Chris. What's wrong?"

"Did you see Jamie before you left?"

"No. Not since that phone call from his dad, to be honest. Is everything okay?"

"I don't know. Thanks, though." He hung up and faced his brother. "She hasn't seen him since his dad's call."

"So he's been missing for two hours?" Cade's eyes widened a little. "That's not like him."

Chris was breaking out in a cold sweat. "Let's see if there's any sign out here before we panic." Though he was barely holding on by a thread.

Splitting up, they walked in different directions. Chris combed the area and the ground, looking for any sign of the younger man. The closer he got to the burned-out shed, the stronger the fading smell of burned wood and other things grew. That would be brought down and cleared by the end of the week, once the insurance adjuster took care of their details. Chris was ready to see it go. Walking around it he studied the pens, but they were empty. "Goddamn it, baby. Where are you?" he muttered under his breath.

Reversing his steps he slowed, taking a wider path around the burnout. The vegetation was growing in thick again after the last rains. They needed to get the tractor back there to keep it cut low. High grass drew in snakes and other small life that they didn't need near the storage shed. Thinking about that, he almost missed the trampled path in the taller grasses.

"Cade!" Chris's heart pounded. His gaze followed the swath of bent and stomped-on grass until he lost it in the distance.

His brother jogged over. "Find something? What the... Do you think he was dragged off?"

Chris handed over his phone. "Call Quade." For the second time that day, he stripped to skin and landed at a full run. His heart had officially migrated to his throat. Chris didn't know what had happened, but he had a bad feeling about what he'd find at the other end of that trail.

Chris followed the trampled weeds and grasses. Jamie's scent was easy to find along the way. There was another's, but Chris didn't know whose. Was he being followed? Dragged? Chris wasn't sure what had happened. Finding Jamie was his only goal.

He took a flying leap over the ravine, his legs pounding the earth. He slowed to a trot to check the ground and then almost rolled to a stop when he didn't find Jamie's scent again. Whirling on his hind legs he backtracked, nose to the ground. Where did he go? He whined, beginning to feel desperate.

*Come on, baby. Where are you?*

It was slow as he retraced his steps to the ravine. Reaching the edge he searched across, then down, and his heart stopped. His legs trembled, threatening to dump him. Jamie lay there, a splayed lump at the bottom. A still and unmoving form. Throwing back his head, Chris howled, long and soulful, alerting Cade that he'd found Jamie.

He leaped to the bottom in two skidding bounds, whining low as he approached. Nearing him, Chris nudged at him, trying to get him to wake. With the way he was stretched it didn't look like anything had broken, though he had some nasty scratches on his arms where his shirt had ripped. It probably would have been worse if he hadn't worn the long-sleeved shirt he seemed unwilling as of yet to relinquish. For that reticence, Chris was grateful.

He licked at Jamie's face, feeling his slow breathing on fur. He almost fainted in relief with that sign. Jamie moaned as Chris bathed his face in licking kisses, urging him back to consciousness.

Slowly, lashes fluttered and a bent leg stretched weakly to straighten. Chris watched as fingers flexed and feet waved. It looked like he was whole, just banged up. He laid down beside him, pressing his back into Jamie's body with his head on Jamie's shoulder, keeping him warm and protecting him until his brothers reached them. He had no choice. There was no way he'd be able to carry Jamie out of the ravine alone.

He panted, forcing a patience he sincerely didn't have.

* * * *

Jamie blinked, bright light disturbing his sleep. He shifted, wanting to roll to his side, but quickly discovered that wasn't happening. "Ow," he moaned, breathing heavily. His shoulder ached. It hadn't before he'd fallen asleep.

Wait. He was in bed and it was bright out? *Crap. Late for work.* How'd he manage that? He reached and searched for the sheets, but he was stopped with a single touch on top of his hand.

"Not on your life, mister."

"Huh?" Jamie swallowed, taking a breath to clear yet more sleep-induced cobwebs. A straw was placed at his lips, and he sipped naturally. It felt good going down, like he hadn't had anything to drink in a while. He sagged onto the bed, feeling like shit. He hadn't felt this bad in a long time. And it was usually after a bad beating from his dad.

Someone he didn't know sat at his bedside when he blinked enough to be able to focus on her. "Who are you?"

"Tina. Don't worry. I'm a friend of Cade's. Let me go get Chris. And don't you dare get up."

Watching her stand and leave, holding a book in her hand, Jamie was at a loss, though he did hurt like hell. When she was gone, he took stock of what was going on. His shoulder ached like no one's business. His arms itched. And he felt like shit. Trying to focus, he'd already noted that. Closing his eyes, he decided it was worth a double mention.

Lying in bed taking an inventory, he discovered he was naked. There were scratches down his arms, and slowly he began to remember. The foot chase. Falling. Scrabbling at the dirt to not fall, then landing with a lung-busting splat. That would explain the shoulder.

"Damn," he said, taking a long breath.

"I swear, I am going to bundle you in bubble wrap if you keep this up." Chris sat in the chair beside the bed. There was clear teasing mingled with deep relief in his admonishment.

Jamie opened his eyes. He hadn't heard the door open. He squeezed Chris's hand when he palmed Jamie's in his own.

"Scared the crap out of me, Jamie. What happened?"

"Someone...behind the shed. Didn't expect him to run." He took a slow breath. "I almost had him, but he jumped and I fell."

"You must have given him a hell of a surprise. That ravine is almost half a mile from the clinic property line."

"Wow," he said a little shocked. Jamie hadn't realized they'd run that far. He was positive he would have caught him too, only once he had, Jamie had no idea what he would have done with him after that.

"Did you find him?"

"No. Quade went back and followed the trail he left. It didn't go much further than where we found you before he lost it."

"Damn." Jamie straightened to stare up at the ceiling. "It was a young man, early twenties. Brown hair. That's all I can remember." He rolled his head on the pillow to focus on the man beside the bed. "Did a dog find me? I remember... But it's so fuzzy."

"We'll talk about that later. You need to rest for a day or two. Nothing is broken, though you're lucky."

Jamie nodded. He wasn't surprised. "Shoulder is killing me."

"I know, baby," Chris said soothingly. He stroked the hand he held, and Jamie started to drift beneath the comfort of Chris's touch. Chris went to place his hand on the bed, and Jamie opened his eyes.

"Don't go," he whispered.

"Do you want me to hold you?"

Jamie swallowed, keeping his gaze on Chris's worried one, feeling the damp in his eyes. He'd never needed this, but from Chris, he *wanted* it.

"Shh. It's okay. I want to."

Jamie edged over on the double bed, for once Cade's size a plus for needing larger than a twin bed. He winced, but didn't complain as Chris threaded an arm beneath him and tucked him into his chest and body. "Rest, sweetheart. I'll be here when you wake up again."

Jamie nuzzled into Chris's throat and pushed away the aches and pains to sleep.

* * * *

Jamie spent the next three days in bed, not that he had much of a choice given that Chris was not going to let him do anything that required more than sitting up in bed or lifting a finger. The day after his fall one of the county police came and took a descriptive report of the guy he'd chased, not that it did much for them considering how little he could give them, but if it was tied to the fires then Jamie was glad to help.

Beyond that? Jamie was ready to gnaw through something to get out of bed for more than the bathroom.

"Chris!" he groaned. "I am fine." He scowled at the gatekeeper sitting beside his bed. "I want to shower." He crossed his arms over his body where he sat, propped against the headboard. The scratches were healing nicely with the constant care he'd been getting. When Chris opened his mouth, he held up a hand. "A real, standing in hot water, shower." Not that he didn't love the washcloth treatment he'd been getting, but enough was enough!

Chris growled in clear argumentative denial.

"I can stand on my own legs for ten minutes," he snapped, approaching impatient with his nurse of the moment. He closed his eyes and concentrated to steady himself. When he opened them he implored, "I have to get back to work. I'm bruised, not broken!"

Chris leaned away in his chair and sighed. "I know." He raked a hand through his hair. "You just gave me a scare. After your dad, and then your fall…" He sought Jamie, begging for understanding.

"Oh, Chris." Jamie opened his arms, and Chris gingerly sank into them to cover Jamie.

Chris nuzzled into Jamie's throat, wrapping his arms around his shoulders to hold him close.

"I'm sorry." Jamie bit at his lip. "I didn't mean to worry you like that."

"I know, baby." After a few minutes of snuggling, Chris said, "Shower with me."

He teethed lightly at the underside of Jamie's jaw, scraping the three day-old rough, which wasn't all that much thanks to his genetics. It's why he didn't let it grow out. If he did, he'd look perpetually sixteen. Between the bites and the idea of showering with Chris, chills were dancing around his spine like tingling kisses. He'd never done that with anyone. It sounded exciting and so very bad that it had to be good.

"Let me spoil you."

A low, rough stutter of a chuckle was impossible to hide. "Chris, you already do. So much."

Chris arched to stare into Jamie's face. Jamie's heart tripped at the heat and caring in his eyes. They shared a sweet, slow kiss while light hands caressed Jamie's face.

Jamie was pretty sure he was falling for the mother hen of the brothers. So when Chris straightened, Jamie said, "First one naked gets soaped first."

## Chapter Eighteen

When Chris jumped off the bed willing to take that dare, Jamie tossed off the covers and shot him a sultry grin. "I win."

Chris laughed, his shirt gripped in fists, slowly lowering at being bested. "Forgot. Sneaky."

"Yup." Jamie scooted to the edge of the bed and stood.

Chris reached out with a hand. Jamie took it without hesitation. What surprised him was when they went across the hall into Chris's bedroom rather than into the bathroom he'd been using. Jamie had been in Chris's bedroom, but hadn't thought much about it as they marched through it without stopping.

"This one is bigger. Had it remodeled when I did the bedroom," Chris told him. He released Jamie just long enough to shuck his clothing and start the water. The bathroom was neat, with fresh-looking pale blue paint and matching tile on the floor and above the sink. The shower was large enough for them with space to spare, walled with brown and gray granite tile and a large shower head on one end. It looked like a guy's bathroom. "Grab some fresh towels." He pointed behind them to a hidden pocket in the wall. After placing two fluffy towels to the side, Chris urged him into the stall, then snapped the door closed.

Jamie sighed as water rained down on them. Chris's hands were gentle and firm on his skin. It felt so good, heat weaving down his body. Most of the stiffness was gone, and there were only spots of soreness. He bowed his head, letting water run like a river down his spine. Thumbs rubbed and circled as he massaged Jamie's back.

"Beautiful, baby," Chris said in sheer appreciation. A soft kiss was gifted to his shoulder, the one he'd landed on. Jamie would never make it as a stuntman. That shit hurt! He moaned, sinking deeper into the caring ministrations he was receiving from Chris. Chris had been wonderful taking care of Jamie, seeing to his recovery from the fall. Thankfully, there had been no more from his dad. He hoped he'd gotten the message that Jamie wasn't coming home, for any reason.

Jamie gasped, a shiver slicing down him when Chris swept his tongue up Jamie's spine. "Ohh," he moaned, gasping.

"Just starting," Chris warned.

\* \* \* \*

Chris roamed Jamie's back with caring hands, mindful of the prominent bruises. Jamie had acquired quite a few new ones, the worst one being on his right shoulder. *Poor baby*. Seemed that just when things were settling for Jamie, life tossed him around again. He skated with massaging hands down his spine, over his ribs, to rub at the dip of his back right above his butt cheeks.

Jamie moaned quietly. Chris leaned forward, pressing a smile into the center of his wet body. A moment later, he filled his hands with the washcloth and soap and began to thoroughly enjoy his journey. Chris hadn't pushed Jamie into more since the afternoon beside the barn, though he'd dreamed of plenty. Seeing his body, lean and taut, it was beautiful. Just what he'd remembered, and then some. Sweet curves and soft skin, tight lines and strong muscle. He could admire Jamie forever.

*Do you love him?* Roman's words echoed through his memory. If love entailed this warmth with being in Jamie's presence, the heat he strived to absorb from his kiss, the urge to be with him that went bone deep, as well as the intense fear he'd felt when he'd gone missing, then Chris would have to admit to himself that he did. Wholeheartedly.

Was Jamie ready for it? He was out from underneath his father's control for the first time in his life. Things were becoming easier for the other man, but not quite settled. Chris had patience. He could care for Jamie, which would be in his favor. Proving that Chris cared by actions when he didn't know if it was right to say the words yet. Chris had never told another those three words. Ed had wanted them. Chris didn't have them then to give.

He watched the soap bubbles dancing in the stream, cascading with the water down Jamie's smooth back. He swallowed the groan, captivated by the sight. The tight globes of his ass flexed and twitched with the swipe of the cloth while Chris's hands molded and formed to skin to follow the paths of white.

"You're amazing."

Jamie shook his head in denial, leaning forward to prop himself against the wall.

"Trust me, baby."

"I do," Jamie said.

Chris almost melted to disappear with the water on the floor.

Focusing again he continued washing, since he'd lost the so-called dare. Down Jamie's legs and then up again. He curled an arm around Jamie's waist, holding him steady as he teased between legs and over Jamie's hole. His entire body quivered in answer. It ratcheted Chris's need higher. He turned him gently, repeating every loving caress and swath down the front, taking special care over his hard cock and beneath. Jamie's length was blush red, the same heated blush of his lips after a thorough kiss.

Chris shook his head minutely, clearing his thoughts. He'd never spent so much time appraising a lover, complimenting them. Adoring them.

*Do you love him?*

*God, Roman. Without a doubt.*

Chris swallowed once, determined to not alarm Jamie with this new whirlpool of enlightenment. "Okay, sweetheart. Under the water."

Jamie obeyed, as malleable as wet clay. Chris circled Jamie's wrists, lifting his arms over his head. "Hold that." He placed Jamie's hands around the shower head. "Don't let go." Jamie watched him through half-open eyes, the blue sizzling with need and want.

Chris worked his palms down Jamie's sides, caressing and kneading at his hips to ease to his knees before him. With firm intention, he widened Jamie's straddle. His dick rose and bobbed in front of Chris's face. Chris licked his lips.

"Chris." Jamie twitched, a shiver that stole over his whole body.

"I lost, right?"

"Oh… Uh…"

Chris had officially made Jamie speechless. He leaned forward to hide his smile. "Consider this part of making sure you're clean."

"Oh hell," he whispered. Jamie's abdomen trembled, proving how hard it was for him to stay still.

Chris moved closer to nuzzle his groin, breathing in his scents, damp musk and clean skin. Jamie's pelvis jerked in answer to the teasing flicks of Chris's tongue. Chris grinned with an evil chuckle. Looking up his taut body, Jamie's head lolled loosely, his lips parted gently as he panted. Jamie's chest rose and fell in sharp bursts, flushed from the warmth of the water and his own desires. Water darkened the hair on his head to a deep golden-honey color. He'd once compared Jamie to an angel. Chris was convinced of it now.

With long strokes he lapped at Jamie's length, feeling it pulse and jump against him, yearning. When he reached the tip, he sipped at the slit with light lips, savoring the fluid waiting for him. He couldn't restrain the murmur of appreciation, bitter but so sweet that Chris craved more. Opening wide, slick skin slipped between Chris's teeth. He groaned, the heat, the sensation, the taste an instant addiction.

Jamie strained, gliding with light force in and out of Chris's mouth. Chris's eyes sank shut.

"Chris. Oh… God, that's so good."

The cock riding his tongue throbbed. Jamie shuddered beneath Chris's fingertips where they curled around his hips. Swallowing hard one more time, the thick shaft popped free when he opened up. Not quite steady he managed to stand, wrapping his arms around a strung Jamie. With two flicks of a hand, the water was shut off.

"I want to make love to you, baby," he whispered, nuzzling under Jamie's ear.

Blue eyes opened with slow-dawning realization. Jamie gulped. One look told Chris everything.

Jamie had never been touched. Shuddering at the impact of that one look, he held him even closer. Roman had said mates were a blessing. That one word didn't even come close to what he felt for Jamie.

"Hang on," he whispered. Jamie soundlessly obeyed, lowering his arms from the shower spout to clasp behind Chris's neck. Pinned together, he maneuvered them out of the enclosed space to stand on the single rug. A quick rub with one of the towels over both of them was the extent of drying them. It wasn't worth the time or attention when compared to what was coming.

Jamie radiated heat. Chest to chest, damp skin had them plastered to one another. Chris backed him out of the bathroom and lowered him to the bed. His throat clogged with surging need, the want to tell him what he felt, with the hunger in his blood and his wolf's desire to claim.

"Never?" Chris breathed, wanting to see the truth in Jamie's pale eyes.

Jamie shook his head, his throat working hard. Lashes fell as he breathed, though by the erratic pounding of his heart against skin he was anything but calm. "Didn't want anyone to see—"

"Shh." Chris lowered from where he hung above him on stiff arms, offering a soft kiss. "I love what I see."

Jamie's gaze flicked upward, his tongue finding his bottom lip for just a second. A cautious hand wound up and over Chris's neck, tugging him down. He could fight it, remain unbending, but he wanted to share everything with Jamie. Their kiss seared Chris. The light duel of tongues, the unhurried plunder, shared, not taken. Chris sighed through a groan when they parted.

"Amazing, now and always."

Red infused Jamie's cheeks. "Show me," he entreated, going boneless between Chris's caging arms. His fingers danced through Chris's hair to trail over a shoulder. He teased the tight tip of a nipple, blue eyes darting back and forth from his touch to Chris's face as he explored.

"That's it, baby," Chris encouraged. He bit his lip to stifle the deepest moans when Jamie pinched him lightly, though he couldn't control the shiver. Jamie studied him, then pushed on a shoulder to roll him over. Chris was dying to feel him, to be one with him, but whatever his baby wanted, he could and would give.

Like the afternoon shared in the grass, Jamie explored him. Teasing with fingers and tongue, teeth and lips. He moved in meandering paths, cutting across nerves with an attentive mouth. Chris watched him as he nibbled and played, and he realized something. Jamie had never had the opportunity to *love* someone physically. Quick peeks through dark lashes proved that he was mindful of Chris's reactions, needed encouragement and direction. Chris felt he was doing well enough not to demean him by choreographing Jamie's efforts.

If anything, he didn't want him to stop. He could live on just this.

A tender palm cupped his sac. Shivers sliced up Chris's body. "Jamie," he managed through a long moan. He moved hair away from Jamie's face to see his eyes. They sparkled with pleasure and sensual heat. "If you're going to do what I think you are, you better plan on sharing."

Jamie blinked at him in confusion.

"Turn around." Chris wiggled his shoulders on the bed and waited.

Slowly Jamie inched around until he was within Chris's reach, then Chris did the rest, hiking his hips to straddle over his body. "That's better," he said in a growl. Then before Jamie had fully grasped what he was intending, he brought Jamie down and started playing with the nuts hanging over him, so plump and ready to be sucked.

"Ohh! Uhh...Chris!" His shout filled the bedroom. Jamie ground down and Chris let him, licking and swirling over the tasty globes. The sweet whimpers and guttural cries drove spikes of need deep into Chris.

Ready to give his lover another taste of bliss, he canted Jamie's body and licked over wrinkled skin. The shout that move garnered had Chris grinning, feeling a flash of pride in making him feel that good.

He paused to catch his breath, and Jamie took advantage of the lapse to engulf his shaft. It made Chris grunt with a suddenness he couldn't hide. He bit at tender thigh flesh, groaning. "Ah, fuck." The ensuing chuckle was sheer evil enjoyment. *My turn,* he promised, then doubled his attack as they volleyed mutual pleasure between them.

His heart pounded. Electricity sliced over his skin. Jamie's light frame shivered when he pressed a finger into the opening he'd just adored. Already slick, he began working one finger, then two, into his silken passage. Shudders rocked Jamie almost nonstop.

More than once he had to stop and uncross his eyes from the torment Jamie was giving his cock. He wasn't going to come this way this time.

As the pressure built, he knew he'd taken all he could and tapped a hip.

Jamie rolled away to his elbow, grinning coyly up at Chris. "Yes?"

Chris shook his head, unable to believe the change in his mate since their first meeting. "Stay right there." He stretched and pulled the lube and condoms from the drawer to drop on the bed. Changing his position before Jamie could adjust, he pinned one of Jamie's knees up to his chest. "Driving me out of my mind is your new favorite thing, isn't it?"

"I'm not saying," he sang. He got a full kiss for the sass. Chris loved seeing Jamie so open and relaxed.

Using the lube, he quickly checked and found that Jamie was ready for him. "Shit, Jamie. That feels…"

"Good," he said in a sigh, his eyes fluttering closed as his body went limp and flat to the bed in welcome surrender. "Don't stop."

Chris quickly rolled on the condom, slicking the cover with extra. With that one leg still held close to Jamie's chest, he leaned forward. He didn't blink as he filled Jamie's heat. With slow care, he disappeared inch by inch.

Jamie whimpered, panting. Then he pushed back against Chris. He snapped his hips, and Jamie moaned. "More. So good."

Chris changed his position, planting Jamie's feet on his shoulders. "Hang on, baby," Chris said, barely able to see through his need.

Lashes lifted, and Jamie nodded. Sultry blue, Chris lost himself in those eyes. He moved, loving Jamie with everything in him. Heart and soul. Jamie panted, gasping and mewling as pleasure mounted and climbed for the both of them. The slide of his cock in Jamie's snug ass was heaven. The smack of skin meeting was a shock to his senses. A slight adjustment between them, and he hit Jamie's prostate.

"Chris!" A full-body shudder rocked the bed.

"Okay?" he asked, slowing with concern.

Jamie grasped at him, nails clawing in desperation. "Now! So close!"

"Do it, baby. Let me see it."

Jamie's hand moved like lightning, stroking his engorged dick with a rapid pace. Two tugs, maybe three, and he cried out. Arching into his thrusts as Chris's balls tightened, the tingling of heat close to the surface. Captured in the slick and satiny grip, his shaft felt every ripple. Then he grunted, losing himself in the volcanic heat that filled his veins and then his dick.

His vision grayed as sparks split his world in two, his wolf howling deep within as the first unbreakable bonds formed. It took several moments to focus, to see the room surrounding them. Releasing Jamie to let his legs sink to the bed he carefully withdrew, watching for any discomfort. It amazed him how little strength he had, ready to collapse in shredded, melted mindlessness.

Removing the condom and tying it off to drop over the side of the bed to dispose of later, he crawled upward and forward to nuzzle into Jamie's body. He rolled Jamie closer. His and Chris's rough breathing were the only sound in the room for some time. At some point he opened his eyes, groggy and feeling a sense of disconnect wrapped in utter bliss. With a monumental effort, he dragged himself off the bed to grab a washcloth and the rumpled towel of their shared shower.

Jamie didn't argue when Chris cleaned him, then himself. After taking care of the towels and the condom, he hefted Jamie into his arms to reposition him on the bed.

The man in his arms wouldn't be sleeping across the hall any longer. Curling beneath the blankets with him, Chris kissed the nape of Jamie's neck, already hearing the deepening of his breathing as he succumbed to sleep. Chris fell asleep pressed against him and touching as much of Jamie as he could, skin to skin.

## Chapter Nineteen

Jamie burrowed into the pillow beneath his cheek. Warm breath eased over his ear, and an arm snuggled him closer to the firm body behind him. Things were starting to get back to normal. He'd gone back to work two days ago. This was his Saturday off. Chris was on-call and last night, he had to go stitch up a calf that got itself trapped in a tangle of barbed wire. Now that Chris was back in bed with him, Jamie lingered. It sounded like Chris was still asleep. Jamie hated that he would be going in for his Saturday shift. All he did was rattle around the house like a ghost when Chris wasn't there.

It wasn't as though there weren't things to do. Feed the horses, then let them out. Keep the house clean, but that only took a little of his morning if that long. Neither he nor Chris was a slob, so it didn't get too bad.

Maybe he'd go wander through town for a little while, go to the library. He hadn't been there yet.

Chris groaned pathetically when the alarm screeched. Arching an arm behind him, he smacked the snooze button. "Hate that thing." He snuggled in closer to Jamie.

Jamie smiled. "You had a long night."

"Uh-huh." He yawned.

"Want me to make you something to eat?"

"That would be awesome." He kissed Jamie's nape.

"Go shower." Jamie was definitely more awake than the slow-moving lump behind him. They usually shared something for breakfast before going in, regardless of whether it was one or both of them. He'd take care of Chris this morning.

"That means moving," Chris grumped.

Jamie nudged him with an elbow. "Come on, lazybones."

Chris nipped him with his teeth, making Jamie squeal and squirm. Just as he settled, the clock repeated its annoying shrill blast.

"Okay, okay," Chris muttered. He rolled away onto his back and found the button to silence the offending destroyer of sleep and snuggles.

Jamie dressed and quickly ran through the bathroom to leave it for Chris. Once in the kitchen, he whipped up some scrambled eggs and toast with bacon. He licked his lips as scents filled the kitchen. Now he was getting hungry.

A few minutes later Chris joined him at the table, clean with damp hair, in his vet scrubs.

"Do you mind if I tag along today? I want to go to the library."

Chris sipped some orange juice. "Course not. You can come and go, use… Oh, I see what you mean." He tipped his head to look at Jamie, a minor frown marring his features. "You need wheels, or something we can share. I use the vet truck for so much, I didn't think about what you could use."

Jamie rushed to point out that he wasn't asking for a handout. "I wasn't putting it out there as a problem for you—"

"I know." Chris finished his breakfast in a couple of quick bites. "But you still need something. Would you like some help looking?" He picked up his plate to rinse it at the sink.

Jamie had expected him to jump in and offer, which wasn't what he wanted. The offer to help him look, though, was much appreciated. Staring at Chris, he got the feeling that Chris knew exactly how far he could go and just how much help he'd take, letting Jamie keep his independence, not to mention his pride. Was it any wonder he adored the man standing at the sink?

"That would be great. You know the areas around here better and know what a good car or whatever has been put through."

"Good. How about next week when I'm not on patient duty?"

Jamie nodded, smiling. Finished with their breakfast, they cleaned up and left for the vet clinic. He snuck a quick kiss before leaving Chris at the clinic. Driving down Main Street into town, Jamie saw the overhead banner touting the coming Fourth of July fireworks and city party.

He pulled into the library to investigate inside. Jamie smiled when the lady behind the counter greeted him.

"Anything we can help you with?"

He shook his head. "Just wanting to look around a bit."

"Okay."

He glanced back and noticed that she was still staring after him as he turned the corner. Jamie guessed that either she knew he wasn't from Silo or they just didn't see that many people at the library on a Saturday. Reading the plaques on the ends of the shelves he roamed the aisles, fingers drifting over spines as he glanced at titles and authors.

Eventually he found the fiction section and began to hunt for a few names that he knew. He'd once been a pretty hardcore reader, but that had dwindled as more and more of his time and energy went into keeping a roof over his and his father's heads.

"Oh, cool!" he cheered quietly. He pulled out one book and thumbed through it happily. A science-fiction thriller he had read years ago. Tapping books, he found the next two in the series. Holding his finds, he needed to see what kind of rules they had on lending.

He placed them on the counter neatly.

"Yes?" the woman said.

"How do I get a card?"

"Are you a resident?" She seemed a little dubious asking him, which wasn't all that unexpected.

He guessed he was now. He nodded, and she handed him an application. It only took a few minutes for his information to be transferred into the computer, then to have a card printed with his name on it.

"Cool." Holding it, he said, "I'd like to get these. Can you get the next three in the series?"

"We can try. I can only do one request at a time."

That wasn't an issue for Jamie. He nodded, saying, "Thanks."

She processed his books and requested the next one. She patted the stack when she was done with them all. "Due in two weeks. And I'm Matilda." She held out a hand, giving him a smile. "Glad to have you here, Jamie."

"Thanks, Matilda." He shook her hand. Since he had the whole weekend off, there was a good chance he'd finish at least one by Monday.

Walking out of the library intending to go tell Chris what he'd found and that he was going home to enjoy them, his feet slowed on the walkway. Looking around, it was quiet. A few cars were parked outside the bakery and down the street in front of one of the clothing stores, but for an early Saturday morning it wasn't very busy at all. Which completely belied the crawl of sensation up his spine. A charged feeling that he was being watched.

Continuing to the truck he scurried a little faster, his head down, though watching through his lashes to try to find the cause of the malevolent weight. There wasn't anyone on the sidewalks, no one skulking behind a tree on the roadside. No loiterers standing within doorways. But there was no doubt. He was being watched.

Sliding into the truck, he did a sweeping search. Finding nothing, he tried to push it out of his thoughts. Away from the library, the clinging feeling didn't follow him. He pulled into a spot at the clinic and then turned off the truck, gazing for a moment in all the mirrors and out the windows. No, no one had followed him. Nothing but trees and pavement surrounded him. He let out a breath. It had to be his imagination. He was a new face in town. Of course he was bound to cause some curiosity, a few stares. It was just as likely that unknown meant distrusted. It didn't mean he had anything to worry about.

After hopping out of the truck, he locked it and went inside. Opening the door, he stepped aside to let out a client with a cat in a carrier. She smiled in thanks and left.

"Hey, Lyla."

"Hi, Jamie. How's your Saturday going?"

He crossed his arms on the reception counter. "Good. Stopped by the library, and now I'm heading home. Is Chris busy?"

"He should be out in a minute or three."

"Okay. I can wait." He stretched over the counter to be nosy and she flat-palmed his face to push him back, laughing at him.

Jamie heard lowered voices, though it didn't register that one of them was Chris's for several seconds.

"I did talk to Roman."

"And he said…"

A sigh. A very rough sigh. "Show him."

Jamie tried to tune it out, not wanting to listen in on a private conversation from another room. He guessed at the angle he stood to the hall that he could hear them, but Lyla couldn't.

"I don't know if I can restrain myself during the next full moon. It's a fight leaving him all night like that."

Jamie tilted his head. Who was he talking about? Who had Chris left alone? The last full moon? He wasn't exactly sure when it had been or when the next one was due. It wasn't unusual for Chris to leave in the middle of the night for an emergency call, so not finding him in bed wasn't a panic situation. But…what if he'd been leaving and it wasn't for a vet emergency? He had been gone for long hours and often came home exhausted. Stifling the urge to twitch he remained impassive and relaxed, though his heart was ticking like a time bomb.

Was Chris looking for a way to tell him he'd found someone else? His throat tightened at the possibility.

"But you're going to have to tell him the truth, Chris."

Chills raked down Jamie's body. That made whatever it was sound even worse, foreboding. There was someone else. Someone that Chris had left Jamie for unaware in their bed. No, not *their* bed. It was still Chris's. He just hadn't known how much it would hurt knowing that Chris didn't want him in the same way, even after everything he'd done for Jamie. After everything they'd done together. It had all been a lie.

"I'm dying to bond with him," Chris said, his wavering voice slipping softly into Jamie's ear. "The wolf is driving me insane, howling and pacing. He's growing impatient…"

Their voices faded, apparently walking toward the back of the hall or the offices to finish their discussion.

Jamie's heart was in his throat. He had to get out of there. "You know what. He's probably tied up on something. Just tell him to call when he's done. I'll pick him up." *If he doesn't already have someone else for that too.*

"Oh, sure. Sorry. I think Quade is back there. Probably yammering on about something about the arson investigation."

Jamie wouldn't have been surprised if that had been the case. Quade was beyond furious over the damage that had been done. Unfortunately, Jamie knew that wasn't what they'd been discussing. Offering a wave, he slipped out the door of the clinic.

He kept replaying the conversation he'd heard. There was something Chris was hiding from Jamie, and it sounded like something big. He didn't understand the wolf comments, and as he rewound and went over it again Jamie was sure he'd misheard something, misconstrued a comment or a meaning. The fact remained that there was something Chris wasn't telling Jamie, was holding back from him. Because Chris knew it would hurt him. He blinked, feeling numb and unsure.

Jamie dug the keys from his pocket and unlocked the truck door. A sharp shove smacked him face first into the frame of the cab. Sparks and pain erupted above his right temple, and he gasped. Trying to turn around to see who was attacking him, he was pounded again into the truck. The sparks faded to gray. Strong arms tossed him over a shoulder, and then everything went dark.

## Chapter Twenty

"Hey, Chris." Quade hung on the clinic door, looking out into the front parking lot.

Chris halted as he led a patient and her twelve-week-old puppy into the exam room. "Yeah?"

"Is Jamie here?"

"No. He went home," Lyla piped up from behind her desk. "Sorry. Forgot to tell you he stopped by. Said he'd be back to pick you up."

"Okay." Chris turned, already dismissing it with his mind on his patient.

"Chris!"

"What?" he nearly snapped, impatient now. He directed Charlotte. "Go ahead inside and set Curly on the table. I'll be right in." Chris twisted, partially closing the door behind him. He was still feeling at odds after the discussion with his brother. The full moon was less than a week away, and this time he wasn't sure he'd be able to appease or distract his wolf by running all night again, exhausting him. He felt the impossible pull of bonding with Jamie growing stronger every minute, every hour, of every day. He'd managed to avoid hurting him by slipping out as soon as he had fallen asleep last cycle. And they hadn't even been sharing the same bed then. With the front door closed between him and then another closed door at his bedroom, once he was wolf there had been no way to reach an unsuspecting and asleep Jamie. It had still been one of the hardest nights of his life, running, but away from the one he needed like air to breathe.

He didn't want to do that again. Chris wanted Jamie to share the full moon runs with him. Wanted him to know his wolf, know his mate. His wolf was digging hard at his subconscious to finish the mating bond. To claim what was his. Now that they'd gone so far as to make love, with the full moon looming...

Chris had been fighting that urge since the moment he'd met the sweet man full of smiles. It was as though the need had become amplified. He was struggling to maintain his control and feared what the cost would be if that control slipped during the full moon.

"The truck is still here," Quade informed Chris with concern. "When did he leave, Lyla?"

Her eyes rounded. "Over half an hour ago."

Quade jumped from out of the doorway and vanished. Chris was hot on his heels, punching through the closing glass door. With Jamie's track record since arriving in Silo, he'd be too happy to find him hanging around outside or doing something where he wasn't immediately visible.

Chris rounded the truck and saw the same thing Quade did. The door hung ajar, the keys were lying on the ground, and there was drying blood on the white frame.

Quade scooped up the keys, carefully avoiding touching anything on the truck. Chris's stomach cinched up tight.

Chris couldn't move. He stood mesmerized by the blood on the paint. Quade lurched out of sight and jogged to the clinic, only to reappear a few moments later. "Lyla called the police."

"Charlotte…" Chris's brain wasn't working at full speed. He couldn't stop staring at the garish red streaks.

"She's handling it. Rescheduling her."

Chris barely heard him. His wolf was snarling and snapping, ready to take action to find Jamie.

It took about fifteen minutes, but a sheriff's car finally pulled in. They filed a report, and the sheriff left.

"That can't be it?" Chris whispered. *A report and a caution to be patient?* His insides were rolling in heaves. He raised a trembling hand to touch a smear of the blood. "Someone took him."

"But who?"

Chris's heart pounded fiercely. Gazing at his brother, feeling like he'd been sucker-punched, he said, "I don't know."

* * * *

Jamie moaned. His head was throbbing. He tried to move, but it only caused him more shooting pain down the side of his head to his neck and beyond. Breathing through his nose he discovered he was gagged, something shoved between his lips and tied securely behind his head. Panic shoved his heart through his ribs, and spots zipped in front of his eyes. He wasn't sure when it happened, but the shock and fear knocked him unconscious.

He awoke to discover that the spinning in his head had eased some, though he had no idea of time or how long he'd been there. He was lying on his side, on a bed. A twitch, a roll of muscles, and he discovered his hands were tied behind his back. He flexed his hands, giving a light tug to his arms. Something was wrapped around his wrists. Fabric. Something he couldn't jerk enough to loosen.

Carefully he slit his eyelids, attempting to see. A wall with a window stretched before him. Heavy drawn curtains. An AC unit hummed and sputtered in the wall beneath it. A hotel room. Where or which one, he had no idea. He didn't even know who had knocked him out. He listened for several minutes, but heard nothing beyond himself. Not another sound. With his eyes closed he did his best to stay calm, ignoring the aching pain attacking his temple.

He faded in and out of consciousness, nausea assaulting him whenever he tried to move too much. *A concussion?* After everything, he now had a concussion. It wouldn't have surprised him.

Eventually the door to the hotel room opened, and he flinched at the band of bright sunlight that flooded the room. He sagged in relief when it closed.

The person in the room didn't turn on any lights, didn't seem to take any interest at all in Jamie hogtied on the bed. Didn't talk to him, either. The deafening grate of locks being turned into place was impossible to miss.

The clank of a couple bottles rattled somewhere nearby and the groan and creak of the next bed filled the cool, dark silence. Then the deep snore of someone passed out eclipsed even the rushed beat of blood against his ears.

Jamie trembled and yanked at the binding on his wrists, but it was no use. He cautiously rubbed his face on the covers, attempting to dislodge whatever was bound around his mouth. Frustration and shooting sparks made any motion a pain-filled nightmare. He had to stop after a few attempts. The pain on that side of his head was intense.

Stretching, he was relieved to discover that his feet weren't bound at least. He tried again to dislodge the mouth gag by working his jaw, but felt almost no give in it. Shifting his focus, he worked his wrists again. Soon even that grew impossible as the aches in his shoulder from lying on one side and the burn of his wrists became too much. Jamie wilted on the bed, quietly swallowing his gasps of pain as to not wake whoever was on the other bed.

The dimness of the room seemed to deepen, either because of nightfall or the shift of the sun elongating the shade on their side of the building, taking away any extra light. He had no idea if the person on the other bed was alone or if there were more people involved, though why they'd kidnap him he had no idea. Painstakingly slowly he twisted to hunt beyond his shoulder, trying to see who was over there.

There wasn't enough light to make out features; nothing more than a lanky man faced away on the bed, sound asleep. He couldn't see any better no matter how hard he tried to slice through the darkness with narrowed eyes. Rolling over onto his shoulder once more, he eased his breathing. At least it didn't look like whoever it was wanted to do something physical, at least not yet.

He closed his eyes to rest, determined to find a way to escape. Jamie wondered if Chris knew he was gone. He'd likely found the truck. They had to know something wasn't right if the truck was still at the clinic but there was no sign of him. At least he hoped Chris suspected that something wasn't right. He had no idea what he could believe after what he'd overheard.

Breathing as calmly as possible, he knew it was up to him to find a way out of this, whatever *this* was.

\* \* \* \*

Chris paced his living room, his stomach a knot and getting worse. There was no sign of Jamie anywhere. Like he'd disappeared in a puff of smoke. Chris had found the library books on the truck seat, and after a quick check knew Jamie had been by there that morning. They'd been able to pinpoint the time he'd vanished to within an hour. That had been that morning. It was dark inside and out now.

His cell phone finally rang, and he jumped.

"Chris? It's Dave. I think we have a lead on Jamie."

Chris almost collapsed where he stood. "Where?"

"Clive Ness used Jamie's bank card at the liquor store."

"His dad?" He lurched to a stiff halt, glaring forward.

"That's what it looks like. Stella caught it when he was there about an hour ago. I just left from talking to her. I have his license plate from the security cameras. I sent it in to Jacob to run. I should have car info in about ten minutes."

"Call me when you have it. We'll help you look."

"You got it." There was a short pause. "We'll find him, Chris." Then he hung up.

Chris's pacing resumed. He called his brothers, and both were ready to begin looking at a moment's notice. When his cell rang again, he almost dropped it in his haste. "Hello?"

"Chris. Roman."

He stopped his intended march out the front door. "I can't talk, Roman. I'm waiting for a call."

His calm tones never faltered, even against Chris's own angst-ridden impatience. "I won't keep you. Call me when you have information. I have three more ready to help you search."

Chris sagged a little at the unending support of his friends and family. "Thank you, Alpha."

"We protect pack, always."

He no sooner disconnected than the phone in his hand rang again. "Dave?"

"I have the car information."

Chris jogged toward the kitchen to write it down. He needed it right to pass the information around. "Ready."

"'97 black Nissan Sentra." Chris wrote down the license plate when Dave rattled it off. "I've already dispatched to the south side of town."

"I'll take the north and get Cade and Quade to do the west."

"East?"

"I'll call Roman." He could put the extra volunteers to use.

"If you find him, call one of us before confronting him."

"I will. And thank you, Dave." His heart was pounding again, but not with so much fear. They would find him.

## Chapter Twenty-One

Paired with Roman driving, they began their search. Every house, every possible street as they hunted in ever-growing circles for the black car. Dave had called Chris not long after he'd teamed up with Roman to tell him the APB had been issued for the car and Clive. Chris didn't care what was done; he only wanted Jamie back, safe and sound.

Rolling slowly down streets, Roman's cell beeped. "Hello? Excellent. We'll call the sheriff. Do not go near his room until one of them arrive." He casually did a U-turn in the middle of the road. "Ben got a confirmation from the night manager at the Comfort Hotel. He has a room there."

Chris was on the phone with Dave before Roman had finished. He shared the information.

"We'll meet you there. Remember, if he's armed, do not approach him."

"Just get there, Dave." Chris ground his jaw.

The hotel was almost ten miles out of town and would have been a far shot for their crawling search.

Dave waited near the front drive in his patrol car as they approached. A second deputy pulled in behind Chris. Roman had sent the few who had been helping home, and Chris was quick to tell his brothers that they were closer to finding Jamie.

Roman put a comforting hand on Chris's shoulder. One of the patrol cars parked behind the

Nissan, and its uniformed driver exited it to look around.

Chris and Roman stood from their car, but stayed back as Deputy Dave Hanlon approached the hotel door. A firm knock received no response. He knocked again. Chris saw the curtain twitch, then slowly the door cracked open.

"What?"

"Mr. Ness? Can you step out for a moment?"

"What for? I was asleep."

Chris heard the way he slurred his words.

"Come back tomorrow." He went to close the door.

Dave put a hand on the door. "Please, Mr. Ness. We would like to talk to you about your son."

"Haven't seen him," he growled.

"I think you have. You used his bank card around seven tonight at Stella's Liquor Store." Dave dropped his hand to his hip holster. Everyone in that parking lot knew Clive Ness did not live in Silo and had no reason to be there, or to be rightfully using Jamie's bank card. "You can come out and discuss it peacefully…"

"Or what?" he demanded with drunken belligerence.

"It would only take about ten minutes to get a search warrant, Mr. Ness," he warned coldly.

"Fine!" He lurched back and jostled the chain on the door. A sober Dave was faster than he was, blocking the door with a stiff arm before Clive could slam it closed. It popped out of Clive's hold, and the whole inside was exposed to the officer.

In less time than a blink of the eye, he had Clive up against the door frame and was yanking his fists together to handcuff them. Chris had never seen Dave move so fast in his life. "Chris. He's on the bed. Make sure your boy is okay. You have the right to remain silent…"

Chris sprinted from where he waited beside Roman through the doorway. "Jamie!" He dived for the bed, pulling him into his arms.

Lashes fluttered, and a deep breath rocked Jamie's chest.

Chris tore at the mouth gag. "Baby. Tell me if that fucker hurt you," he snarled lowly.

Jamie gasped, sucking in air when the rag was ripped away. Chris leaned Jamie into his chest to attack the loops over his wrists. Jamie sagged into him like he didn't have a bone in his body. "I got you, baby. You're safe." He blinked when someone turned on the lights, but it didn't slow him down. Roman came to stand by the bed.

"Jamie?"

He moaned, limp in Chris's arms when he was finally loose. He wasn't moving, hadn't said anything.

Holding him close, Chris saw the trail of blood on his scalp where it had dried against his temple. "He needs to go to the hospital."

"I'll drive you," Roman offered, calm as always.

Chris didn't think to debate it. Jamie's head needed to be X-rayed. He bundled him into his chest and carried him out of the room. Dave was just getting Clive into his cruiser.

"I'm taking him to the hospital," Chris announced. Dave only nodded.

He knew Dave would be in touch, but Jamie was his only priority. He doubled over to settle them both on the car's backseat, not letting Jamie go for a second. Roman closed the door behind them, then sat behind the wheel.

Chris crooned to and petted an unconscious Jamie the entire drive to Stiller Springs.

Within minutes of arrival at the ER, Jamie was whisked away to be examined and have X-rays completed. Chris dropped into one of the waiting chairs. He knew it, without a doubt, that his entire life had just disappeared into the hospital's innards.

* * * *

Jamie moaned, lifting a hand toward the throbbing in his head. Gentle fingers caught him and held him still.

"Shh, baby. You're safe."

Jamie blinked, focusing in the unknown room. His memories were a jumbled mess. Light strokes on his arm eventually registered, and he twisted in that direction. "Chris?"

"I'm here."

"What... Where am I?"

"The Stiller Springs hospital. They wanted to keep you until you woke up. You have a concussion."

Jamie's eyes closed. For some reason, that didn't come across as a surprise. Then he remembered *how* he'd received that concussion. "Dad!"

Chris brushed his fingertips over his forehead to soothe him. "Is spending the night courtesy of the county with Deputy Hanlon."

Jamie squinted in confusion. His vision was a little blurry, and he was so tired. The room was thankfully dim, but his head still throbbed like an entire college dorm was having a midnight party.

"He's in jail. He's been charged with kidnapping, robbery, and a few other things."

Jamie managed a weak nod.

"Go ahead and rest, baby. They won't let you out until morning."

"Stay?"

"All night."

Jamie drifted off, still holding Chris's hand in his.

\* \* \* \*

Jamie opened his eyes slowly. He did a cautious check from one hand to the other and all the parts in between. Except for the pain behind his eye, he seemed to be mostly in one piece. He let his lids droop, then he heard the low tones of Chris's conversation and realized he wasn't at his side where he'd been when Jamie had fallen asleep.

"Thank you, Roman, for everything. Yes, I'm going to. As soon as we get home. I can't take it anymore. I just pray—" Jamie heard the way his voice trembled. "I can't lose him. If he can't accept my wolf, I'll have to keep trying."

Jamie watched as Chris paced in clipped circles at the end of the bed, his cell phone at his ear. The sun wasn't up yet, so Chris probably thought he was still asleep.

His head continued to ache, though it was a low-grade throbbing now. He noticed they'd removed the IV drips during one of the many nurse check-ins. He didn't miss them in the least. Maybe that meant he would be out of there soon.

Jamie followed him through lowered lashes as Chris disconnected the phone call and paused to run a hand over his face. He looked exhausted, worn out to the core. Had he been here all night?

Jamie swallowed, trying to talk, and actually managed a rough few words. "Did you sleep at all?"

Chris spun on a dime and was back by his bedside. "A little," he whispered. "How do you feel?"

"A little worse for wear," he said, trying to smile. Whatever they'd been giving him to ease the throbbing headache still made him feel groggy.

Chris chuckled. "You have a high tolerance for pain if this is your idea of a little." He scooped up Jamie's hand. "Can't wait to get you home, baby. The doctor will be by after seven, so we have a couple hours yet."

His gray eyes barely blinked, staring at Jamie like he was Chris's whole world. Jamie steadied himself. "What is it you've been hiding from me, Chris?" he asked. When Chris angled upward in shock Jamie held his hand tighter, keeping him right where he was. "Who is it you want me to meet?" He licked dry lips. "Is there someone else?"

"Of course not," he said, coming close to nuzzle into Jamie's chin. "I love you."

Jamie gasped, his fingers tightening on the hand he held. "You love me?"

"Heart and soul, baby." Chris straightened, giving him a sweet smile. Cupping the hand he held in his own tender palms, he kissed knuckles and fingertips. "Love you like you live inside of me," he said.

"Then what is all the..." Jamie waved a little loop with his free hand.

"Wolf talk?"

"Yeah."

Chris dropped his gaze, then his chin. "It's something I need to show you." He rubbed tiredly over his eyes with stiff fingers. "You said you remembered waking up in the ravine and seeing a dog, right?"

Jamie nodded.

"And you saw a dog playing with Tiberius."

Jamie repeated his answer. He couldn't remember now if he'd ever mentioned it, but he must have if Chris knew. Maybe he'd seen it from inside the barn that day after all.

What Chris said next couldn't have been heard right.

"That wasn't a dog, Jamie." Chris swallowed. He twisted away, a harsh grimace hardening his features. "I've never told anyone else, Jamie. You are the only one who is *born* to know this." He firmed his lips, then let out a sharp exhale. Gray eyes became bright as he stared right at Jamie. "It's going to be hard to believe, but once we're home I'll be able to prove it to you. I'm a shape-shifter. I can change into a wolf."

Jamie gaped at him. He tried to tug his hand free, and Chris caged him.

"Jamie," he pleaded. "Just…try to understand."

He shook his head. The rush of his heart accelerated the pounding against his temples. Closing his eyes he drooped to the pillow, unable to go far or escape.

A gentle hand swept over his forehead. "Rest, baby," Chris said. An aching overtone made his voice hoarse. "No matter what, I love you."

\* \* \* \*

Chris wrapped a hand around Jamie's waist, aiding his slow walk up the path to the front door from Cade's truck. Very little had been said between them since that morning's conversation, and the longer the silence stretched the more worried Chris was becoming. He didn't know how to *stop* worrying.

Cade carried the small bag of clothes he'd brought to the hospital that morning for Jamie's release. It had all been…mechanical. The doctor. Explanations. Care and recuperation for the next few weeks.

It seemed like ever since Jamie had arrived, he'd been hurt or banged up in one place or another.

Chris nodded in thanks when his brother unlocked the door ahead of them. Chris directed Jamie to the couch and let him slide down to sit. "Okay?"

Jamie's blue eyes drifted away, and he nodded.

"If you need anything just call, okay?" Cade was leaning toward the door. Chris was sure the tension between himself and Jamie was making his brother uncomfortable.

"Thanks for everything, Cade."

"Thank you, Cade," Jamie murmured, sliding him a single look.

"You're both welcome. Rest up, Jamie."

That earned Cade a slightly warmer smile in answer from Jamie. Cade waved and closed the door on his way out.

Chris knelt on the floor at Jamie's side. "How is your head? Do you need anything?" When Jamie didn't answer, he leaned in to search his closed expression. "Are you mad at me? What can I do?"

"I don't know," he admitted. "I can't figure out why you lied to me—"

"I didn't lie, baby."

His jaw ground back and forth. "Then… Okay. The wolf story." Accusing disbelief.

Chris grazed the side of Jamie's face with the back of his hand, a winsome caress. "Let me just show you. It's the only way to prove it. Will you give me this chance?"

Jamie studied his clasped hands in his lap. "Not going anywhere fast."

"You are not trapped, Jamie. You are not my prisoner. You never have been." Chris rolled his shoulders to lean away. "Just watch and know that I love you."

Standing to his feet Chris stripped, laying his clothing on the couch beside a suspicious Jamie. "I'm sharing my family's deepest secret with you, Jamie. It is not contingent on how you feel for me, though I hope you do care." *I also hope I'm not about to lose the best thing in my life.*

Bare to the skin, he took three large steps away to stop in front of Jamie, more so he wouldn't feel threatened when a full-size male wolf stood before him. Fear unlike anything he'd ever known chilled him, rose inside from Chris's center, because of the absolute hollowness of Jamie's gaze.

"I will explain everything after this. I promise."

Chris refused to crack beneath the cynical expression on Jamie's face. Jamie leaned into the couch and waited. Waited to call his bluff.

Only it wasn't a bluff. Not by a long shot.

Chris closed his eyes and called on the wolf, who was too happy to be out and in his mate's presence. The bend in his legs took him to the floor quickly, his spine compacting as his head broadened and his jaw lengthened. It didn't hurt anymore, not at his age, but Chris knew it was disconcerting for someone to hear the changes happening, the bones realigning. Shaking himself to settle his coat, he searched for the man on the couch. The one man outside of his family and pack who would know him inside and out. Chris kept a firm hand on the scruff of his beast, and four paws danced in place in anticipation on the wood floor. A soft whine was the only dissent to Chris's relentless control as both waited for a reaction from Jamie.

## Chapter Twenty-Two

Jamie didn't know what to think. Not even a moment ago, Chris, his boyfriend, had been standing naked in the living room.

A near-coal-black wolf now stood in the exact same spot. Thick fur coated him from his neck to his tail. The same gray eyes he'd known for months met him stare for stare. Jamie was gaping at him—it—in the face, but it wasn't...it didn't...seem real. How could this be real? *Hallucination? Concussion? Sure, anything is possible.*

*This. Is. Not.*

Jamie raked his tongue over the roof of his mouth. His throat clicked when he swallowed, it was so dry.

The curious tilt of a lupine head prompted the image of the dog playing with Tiberius into his memory. It was the same gesture the animal had used to egg on the horse.

Jamie's hands gripped into each other tighter, camouflaging their shaking. "That was you," he managed, unable to hide the quiver.

The animal's head bobbed in answer, then dipped, imploringly.

"You can understand what I'm saying, can't you?"

Another answer. His soft gray eyes had hardly blinked since he'd taken on the shape of…of…

"Holy shit," Jamie cursed quietly. Flexing his fingers, he released his own death grip and scrubbed over his face, especially his eyes. The click of nails on the wood floor sounded odd in the quiet home. Jamie slid his hand a fraction lower, seeking the source of that sound over it. "No. Stay there," he quickly stated.

The wolf stopped with still a foot between them. Stopped cold. He ducked his head and whined.

"This is real," he murmured. "I'm not still in the hospital imagining this."

The wolf sat and tilted its head to stare at him, panting. A long tongue lolled out the side of its mouth, a powerful mouth fully loaded with sharp teeth. Jamie followed that tongue and the animal it belonged to when it slurped and continued to pant.

"Chris?" Jamie managed a faint whisper.

The wolf perked up. Standing, it wasn't exactly wagging its tail, but it didn't seem at all threatening.

*Uh-huh, and volcanoes don't burn.*

Jamie inched across the couch, away from him. That unblinking stare never left him. The rush of his heart was making his head throb, pulsing blood through his body at an accelerated rate. One he doubted was helping his concussion situation any.

"Just…just stay there, okay?" Jamie didn't stop moving, slowly widening the gap between him and… Jamie swallowed. That wasn't Chris. Jamie didn't know *what* that was. He was dreaming, or hallucinating. Chris didn't have fur. He walked on two legs, not four, and definitely did not have inch-long steak knives for teeth.

The animal's head swiveled, following him, though it did as he'd asked. It wasn't coming closer. Jamie cautiously stood with the aided push of a hand on the couch's armrest. He wobbled and reached for the wall.

The wolf raised a paw, his attention riveted.

"No. No. Stay," Jamie managed. His ears were ringing.

The animal whined, but its paw sank to touch the floor again.

Jamie crept around the corner of the hallway, always keeping the gaze of the animal before him, until just his head would have been visible around the corner.

"Don't move," he repeated, not caring if he was understood or not. That was *not* Chris. His mind was playing tricks on him.

When there was a broad enough gap, he whirled and tore through the door of what had once been his bedroom. The wall shook when he slammed it tight, locking it for good measure, to lean against its smooth surface. His heart was doing its best to become a permanent part of his sternum.

Drawing a much-needed breath, he raised a hand and cupped the side of his head. He felt woozy.

"Jamie?" Chris's concerned voice seeped through the door.

Jamie sagged, practically melting into a blob on the floor.

"Jamie, please. Talk to me." There was a very long pause, then, "Just let me know you're okay. Say something. You're scaring me, baby."

"Is... Is it gone?" He wrapped his arms around his middle, shivering.

"Yes. It's gone."

Jamie couldn't place all the emotions in Chris's answer, three little words.

There was a soft thud, like he'd dropped his forehead to the door. "I'm sorry, baby. I didn't want to scare you." Aching hollowness permeated every syllable.

Jamie twisted to rest against the door, his chin nearly on his own shoulder. He couldn't break down everything that had just happened. It was beyond impossible.

"I'll leave you alone." Chris sighed. "If you... If you want to talk, or...anything, I'm here. I need to go check on Bear and Biscuit." A light shuffled noise proved he was doing as he said, leaving Jamie in peace, but before he had completely left Jamie heard, "I will love you, no matter what." The soft pad of bare feet faded and Jamie closed his eyes, willing the tremors to stop.

* * * *

Chris tore open the closest hay bale, pitching chunks into stall feeders in his anger. He'd let a grateful Tiberius and Biscuit out of their stalls when what he really wanted to do was scream, howl, or run until he couldn't feel.

The last thing he'd expected had been total rejection. Disbelief he could change. Trust he could win.

Unwillingness to accept? He couldn't begin to touch that until Jamie was talking to him again. He'd had no choice but to leave him in his room. Forcing it would have won nothing.

Hauling around the wheelbarrow and shovel he began cleaning the horse stalls, a tedious mind-numbing labor, but it was a distraction he would have paid good money for at that moment.

And it wasn't just him who was disappointed. His wolf was upset. He didn't even get close enough to touch. Jamie's scent had been an aphrodisiac, an aromatic that called to his baser instincts. *Mate.* His wolf knew it, and Chris was trying to help Jamie see it.

Except he wasn't doing a good job of it.

At first, he thought Jamie was taking it well. The change wasn't instantaneous or uneventful. Taking the wolf's shape wasn't something he could pretend didn't happen. Jamie hadn't run from the room, shrieking in terror, and had even spoken to his wolf, had called him by name. Then…

Chris sighed, wiping a hand across his damp brow. Maybe it was the injury making him believe he'd imagined it all. Chris didn't know. All Chris wanted to do was hold him, tell him everything would be okay. He knew he'd have to take this slow. It just looked like it was going to be closer to a crawl to help Jamie understand.

Which meant bonding with him was not going to happen anytime soon. He rested his head on bent forearms, where they teetered on the tip of the shovel handle. The full moon was days away. He'd have to sneak out again. He hated being deceitful, not even telling Jamie he was leaving, gone for hours. He scrubbed his eyes over his shirt sleeve. Worse, Jamie thought there was someone else. That gutted him. There would *never* be anyone else.

"Chris?"

Run with the Moon

He spun, gripping the shovel so it didn't clang to the ground. "Hey," he said as evenly as he could.

There was a little jump of his heart, finding Jamie standing only a few feet away. He looked tired and a little pale. Chris imagined there was some pain, even if Jamie wasn't showing it. He'd been warned the same as Jamie that headaches would come and go for the next few days. The problem to watch for was the worsening of either. Chris really hoped there wasn't a setback so Jamie could heal quickly. His baby had been banged up so much, Chris had no idea how he was staying so resilient to it all. He was dressed in jeans and a loose T-shirt, what he'd worn home from the hospital. Sexy, sweet, and adorable.

"How is your head?"

"Ringing, but I'm not seeing double." He made an attempt at a quirked smile.

"You should probably go lie down, at least until tomorrow."

Jamie put his hands in his pockets, then ducked his head. "I will." His tongue poked out and touched his lip. "Look, about…earlier."

Chris leaned the shovel against a stall wall and forced his feet to not take a step closer, watchful of Jamie's reactions. He didn't want to crowd him, but he was dying to touch him, to comfort him.

"You…" Jamie sucked in a sharp breath and looked upward to the barn rafters. "You said you'd talk about it."

"I meant that." A small tremor ricocheted through Chris's body, a cautious flare of hopefulness.

Blue eyes narrowed to pierce him when it seemed he'd found his strength. "What are you?"

"Rare," he admitted truthfully. "The ability is passed from father to child. Women can have the ability, but they can't give it to a born child."

"So…"

"Yes, all three of us."

Jamie raised a hand and rubbed stiff fingers across his forehead. "How many are there?"

"Here? Not quite twenty. There are communities worldwide but it's kept very quiet, and no one knows of all the branches."

Jamie's arms cinched close to his sides protectively. His gaze implored Chris. "It's just…"

Chris waited. He wanted to scoop him up so badly, hold him close. He didn't so much as twitch.

"Insane," Jamie finally whispered. "Seriously. How do you stay hidden? How do you do what you did?"

"The first isn't easy," Chris admitted. "The second? We learn, like walking or riding a bike."

It felt like an eternity passed as they stared at each other. Chills shook Chris's frame as they remained frozen in place. He didn't dare make the first move. His patience and hope were rewarded when Jamie slid his hands out of his pockets and took a very small step forward. Chris knew just how hard that step was to take. Daring to believe the unbelievable.

Cautiously, Chris raised a hand as an offering. And waited. Jamie reached forward, and Chris cleared the gap between them to tenderly take Jamie in his arms. He sighed a breath of relief so deep, he felt limp when Jamie tucked into his shoulder and wrapped firm arms around Chris's waist.

"I'm so sorry for scaring you." He moved a fraction closer and kissed the bruise on Jamie's temple, the lightest pressure of adoration.

"Shocked me. I still don't understand."

"I know." After a minute, Chris lifted Jamie to look into his eyes. "There is no one else. Just you." He cradled a trembling Jamie into his chest. "When you disappeared yesterday morning, my entire world went with you."

Jamie bit at his lip, insecure and uncertain, as though absorbing everything Chris was telling him. "Is it safe?"

"My wolf? Safer than a declawed kitten to you. He's me, in many senses of a symbiotic relationship, and I'd never hurt you."

Chris didn't push, though he craved to know Jamie's thoughts. Chris had told him when he'd awakened in the hospital last night that Jamie was his everything, that he loved Jamie completely and fully. Jamie, as of yet, hadn't said the same. He was hoping that bringing the wolf out hadn't destroyed any of Jamie's feelings.

Exposing the truth was inevitable, regardless of the risk it had been. He couldn't continue to hide half of his being if he wanted Jamie. And the wanting was without question. He would take this as slow or as fast as Jamie could handle it.

Jamie nuzzled in tighter, forming to Chris's chest.

"Let's get you into bed for a while. You need to rest for a couple of days, at least."

Jamie sighed with a hint of forlorn acceptance. "It's a good thing my boss is so understanding. Looks like I'll be missing work again."

Chris brushed his lips to Jamie's temple and cheekbone. "I'm sure he doesn't have a single problem with it."

Jamie rubbed his nose against Chris's shirt, hiding, but Chris easily felt the lighter smile through the fabric of his shirt.

## Chapter Twenty-Three

Jamie pushed the grocery cart while Chris walked at his side tossing in things as they came up on the list. After a couple days of inactivity and a very watchful boyfriend, he was ready to get back to work. Jamie's assessment of Chris, tagging him as the mother hen of the brothers, had been on the mark. Chris had hardly let him out of bed, and there hadn't been anything between them beyond a few sweet kisses. He was about to scream in frustration at the man.

He'd been doing his best to not think too hard on the…other thing. They really hadn't talked much more about it. Jamie guessed that Chris was letting him come to it at his own pace. For that, he was grateful.

Turning down another aisle, a familiar face smiled at them. "Hey, Jamie. How are you feeling? Cade told me you had a run-in with your dad." Tina gave him a gentle look of understanding sympathy.

"I'm doing okay. He's in jail. He hasn't been able to raise bail."

She frowned and shook her head. "I'm sorry for speaking against your father, but he deserved it for what he did to you." She leaned on a hip, holding her own cart in front of her.

Jamie wasn't going to argue. The man in jail didn't resemble the father he'd once thought of as an actual parent. It wasn't any wonder he hadn't recognized him in the dimness of the hotel room. He'd lost a lot of weight, making his usually robust frame seem lanky and bony. Apparently losing Jamie had cost him more than just money. That wasn't any kind of reason though for him to come after Jamie to try to get it.

"Going running tonight, Chris?" Tina asked, shifting attention.

"I don't know yet. If I'm there, you'll see me."

"You should bring Jamie. I know everyone is curious about meeting him. I feel special." She winked at Jamie. "I've seen you naked." She giggled, waving fingers at him. "Just playing. I know you're Chris's to the core." She grabbed the cart bar. "Okay. Time to get back on track. See you guys later." She smiled and trotted off, holding a clipped list in one hand.

"Running?" Jamie asked, though he was pretty sure he knew. His throat was a little dry as he was smacked with the reality of what Chris was all over again.

"Every full moon, the pack gathers to run," he explained quietly. "I'll tell you more when we leave." He glanced around, making the point that there was no privacy for them. Jamie nodded. The time spent finishing the shopping would give him a chance to prepare for whatever it was Chris was going to share.

* * * *

Chris settled the last bag on the backseat of the truck. Jamie had already climbed in on the other side and buckled up. He noted that Jamie was faced away from him, withdrawn and deep in his own thoughts. His behavior wasn't giving Chris a very optimistic feeling about what was coming. He hadn't really made the full decision to go that night to run. He knew he needed it, knew his wolf did too. Needed to bond with his pack and feel the earth beneath his paws. Needed to just play without the stress of life strangling him. Yet he was more than willing to ignore all those needs if Jamie wasn't ready.

He blew out a quiet breath and then closed the half-door to the backseat. He inserted the key into the ignition once behind the wheel and waited. "Talk to me, Jamie," he said, trying to hide his nervousness and anxiety.

Jamie's fingers flexed, fisted, then relaxed to spread out on his own thigh. "I'm not sure how."

Chris's lungs hurt as he fought to find air. He felt it, the rift this was causing them. He closed his eyes and fortified his efforts. He couldn't lose Jamie. Not now. Not after everything they'd been through. The thought of going on without him flayed Chris from the inside out.

"I am trying to understand," Jamie reiterated.

Chris stared out the windshield to the parking lot. Other cars did nothing to distract him. "How can I help?" *Please let me help, baby.*

Silence seemed to fill the cab of the truck with an oppressive weight. Sunlight beat down on them from a cloudless sky. He started the truck just to get the AC flowing. After an interminable moment of silence, Chris put the vehicle in drive and left the grocery store.

Jamie's voice broke the silence unexpectedly. "Take me with you." Firm but quiet.

"Tonight? Running?" Chris's heart slammed into his ribs. He had *not* anticipated that.

Jamie's jaw firmed, his lips doing the same. He nodded. "Yes. Tina said they want to meet me. I won't be in danger from them, right?" He swept his eyes up once, a quick glance that was a merest peek at blue, before they were stolen away again. "You wouldn't let them hurt me." It was said clearly, but there was a hint of question. Like he wanted to believe it, but…

"No, Jamie. No one will hurt you." He swore he would die before any of the pack so much as put a scratch on him. "You've already met our alpha. Roman has approved you so anyone who doesn't like it will have to answer to him first as pack leader, then me as your mate. You are protected."

"Roman?" he murmured with a hint of surprise. He shook his head a minute or two later. "Should have guessed. I can see it now."

They drove beneath the banner for the Fourth of July celebration that weekend. He noticed that Jamie read it as they went beneath it as well, a hint of longing in his expression. Chris would make sure they went just to spend time together. Jamie was already a part of so much of his life. He realized he wanted to do everything with him.

A flashback of his mother's pain over his father's death made so much more sense to him now. Clammy hands wound around the steering wheel as he drove. He would fall apart if he lost Jamie, and they weren't even bonded yet. After? It would kill him—instantly—if anything happened to him. It was almost terrifying to realize how much of his life was now wrapped up in this man's care.

"When do you go out?" Jamie's question brought him back to the discussion at hand.

"Roman will call with a meeting place tonight. It's never known beforehand, so the chance of discovery is minimal. I tell him then if I'm attending the run. If you're expected but don't show, he will check on you. Safety and secrecy are key to our survival. We have lost pack, but never on a running night."

"Like your parents?"

Chris motioned stiffly. "Yeah. We all think there was a poacher. We can heal, but certain wounds are still fatal. Dad made it home, but he didn't survive."

Jamie reached out and settled a gentle hand to Chris's thigh. No platitudes, just comfort. Chris covered his palm and gave him a squeeze in thanks.

"And others?" Chris felt the fine tremor in the palm he held within his own. "Their...mates?"

"All are welcome. Some come to keep others company while the pack is running. Some come to be with their lover, to share in the run and play." He'd probably get a hard reprimand for this if it was ever learned he'd said it, but he added, "It's like being surrounded by a large group of puppies." No shifter wanted to be compared to a puppy, but their antics *could* be described as such. Just not to their face.

A smile danced over Jamie's lips. "Hard to be scared of puppies."

"Like any other situation, trust is earned as they become familiar with you, animal or person."

There was a twitch, a perceptive play of fingers in the hand still caged within Chris's. "I understand."

Jamie raised his chin to stare out the side window again as they drew closer to Chris's house. A house he desperately wanted to make theirs.

"Okay. I want to be there. If you want me to be," he finished softly, quickly, like Chris could or would deny him.

Chris stopped in front of the house to then reach across the seats and unbuckle Jamie and himself with a single-minded focus. He slid Jamie's frame across the seat and into his chest. His heart raced a tattoo into his ribs when Jamie looped his arms around Chris's shoulders, gazing up into his face when he stilled.

Chris's voice was hoarse with emotion, unable to hide all the swirling feelings inside. "Baby, I love you. I want you with me every minute I breathe. This was something that I had to leave up to you, though. It goes against everything that we believe in as sacred to force a mate to accept us." He ran a tremulous hand into Jamie's curls above his ear. "It can ultimately lead to expulsion from a home pack if you mistreat or abuse your mate." He touched forehead to forehead, searching those blue eyes that he realized with a hard thud of reality owned him heart and soul. When exactly that had happened, he didn't know, but he couldn't deny it, either.

Jamie searched him closely. "I don't want to lose you. Just...give me time."

"All you want." He lowered, and as tenderly as possible, swept over inviting lips.

Jamie all but melted, molding to Chris's embrace as sweetly as any he could remember and better than any of those same memories. He hadn't said anything yet about his feelings. Chris was doing his best to keep his impatience from getting the better of him. Jamie wanting to know, to share in his pack said a lot, even if he couldn't say the words yet.

Both were breathing a little more heavily when Chris released him. "Let's get this stuff inside," he said. Then he wanted to kiss Jamie to within an inch of his life. He loved the way Jamie pressed against his body, angle to angle. Like he wanted to touch and get as close as Chris did.

Jamie nuzzled into Chris's chin and neck, gifting a gentle kiss to his rampant heartbeat. It all gave Chris hope that the coming night's run wouldn't end in disaster.

## Chapter Twenty-Four

Chris wasn't expecting it when, after folding the last grocery bag to go into a keeper in the pantry, Jamie tackled him up against the kitchen counter. He gasped, one hand reaching to brace himself with the other encircling Jamie's waist to steady them both.

"If I'm going tonight, does that mean you're done treating me like I'm going to break?" Jamie demanded with a throaty growl.

Bright eyes pinned Chris as much as his body did to the unforgiving solidness of the counter. The roughness of both his actions and Jamie's voice shot chills down Chris's spine.

Chris squeezed his fingers, bringing Jamie even tighter into his frame. "Didn't want to hurt you more," he explained. Though the way Jamie was rubbing into him, a full-frontal glide of seduction, wasn't making speaking easy for him.

"I am going to work tomorrow," he pointed out between nips to Chris's throat, in a *try to stop me* manner. "That means I'm okay."

Chris's eyes unfocused, his thoughts quickly going the same way. It had been so long since he'd given in and loved on Jamie. It looked like Jamie had taken the reins and was going to prove he was well enough for sex. *Oh shit.* He moaned silently when the bite of teeth found flesh and hung on.

Chris was dying. He couldn't keep up with every little thing Jamie was doing to him. Fingers had snuck beneath his T-shirt and were at that moment scoring paths over ribs and muscle. Tingles were bursting in his wake. Then his shirt was being yanked forcefully upward. Chris aided him, not concerned as Jamie tugged it free and away. He'd find it later.

Chris had barely caught his breath when his jeans were split wide open and dropped. "Jamie!"

Sharp teeth bit at tender skin right at the top of his pelvis, and Chris's head snapped back on his neck. "Fuck!"

Blood rushed and hardened his length, making him dizzy with the sudden drop of blood pressure south. He gripped the kitchen counter with clawed fingers just to stay upright. Jamie's hands were everywhere. Skimming and teasing, pleasing and roaming. Those same hands used his butt cheeks as hand holds as he dived nose-first into Chris's groin. He hissed, awash in sensation. He didn't have a single clue of when Jamie had sunk down in front of him onto the floor.

A firm palm gently supported his aching shaft, giving Jamie room to pop the crown between waiting lips. Shivers rolled over Chris in a storm. Sound vanished. He was barely breathing. He whimpered, braced blindly to the counter as Jamie used his mouth like a weapon to destroy any sense of reality. He'd learned that first encounter that Jamie knew what he was doing when it came to sucking dick, and he wasn't shortchanging Chris this time, either.

Diana DeRicci

Rough pants were the only sounds in the kitchen, the only sounds in his ears for several minutes. Slow hums and pleased murmurs added to the musical rhythm. Chris moaned, a whine really, when a fingertip danced over his opening. He spread his legs wider, wantonly begging and not caring. Jamie gave him what he wanted, gently breaching through the muscle. Chris was positive his legs were going to give out on him. Shocks sliced up his frame. Sweat broke out on his skin, the urge to come beating at him as Jamie constantly increased the pleasure plateau.

"Jamie." Chris growled his name.

A pop filled the surrounding quiet when Jamie released him. He slunk upward, his tongue weaving a damp path over Chris's skin. "Do you trust me?"

Chris uncrossed his eyes, gulping air to gaze into Jamie's expectant face. "Always."

Jamie took a step back and offered a hand. Chris placed his palm in it without question. Jamie surprised him by simply walking him forward to encourage him to lean over the dining table. Chris looked over his shoulder. And swallowed. He braced his hands flat, but didn't raise himself more than to keep a watchful eye on Jamie. Anticipation swirled with the surprise. His body actually ached and shivered with want.

He let Jamie finish undressing him, stripping his jeans and shoes to leave him utterly naked and on display at the table.

"I know I've never really said it, Chris, but you are amazing. Can't stop from touching you, don't want to," he said with a reverent undertone. Palms swept from the top of his ass upward to his shoulders, a strong caress that loved as well as enflamed.

Chris closed his eyes and stretched his arms out to grip either side of the table. Something he'd never done for another was utter surrender. It went against the will of his wolf to be submissive, but he knew Jamie would never hurt him. In fact, he was very willing to bet what he was going to be feeling was pleasure unlike anything he'd ever known.

"I want you to, Jamie." *Fuck me, mate. Love me. Make me yours.* He sighed, closing his eyes to rest a cheek on the tabletop and wait. Nerves sizzled with unbridled anticipation.

\* \* \* \*

Jamie stood in shock as Chris simply went pliant to rest on the table. He'd never expected that kind of acquiescence to his request. The action made him rock hard in his jeans. He ripped his shirt off and let it fall to the floor. Standing behind Chris he leaned forward, brushing their bodies together, teasing while he ran exploring palms up and down his sides and shoulders. "Love the way you feel." He kneaded at taut firmness, drowning in the way Chris's muscles bunched and trembled for him.

"Love you touching me," Chris rasped. He lay still and vulnerable with his eyes closed and a cheek pressed flat to the table. Almost as though chains held him down, he didn't move an inch. Trusting in everything Jamie was doing to him.

Knowing how deep Chris's need to take care of Jamie went, the absolutely malleable male before him drove him wild. He *needed* this man. They still had a lot to work through, but he couldn't deny the depth of feelings that he hadn't allowed himself to face until then. So much had happened since he'd come to Silo, since Chris had found him on the side of the road. He'd learned at an early age to not take much for granted, but he was beginning to think that what he had with Chris was real, was that forever kind of love—

Jamie froze, his hands stilling on the broad back in front of him. It hit him with a rather overwhelming impact. He loved Chris. Deep, to the core. It wasn't one of those roses-and-hearts kinds of love, but one built through time and trust. A need for each other that went more than skin deep. He bit back the raw sound that almost escaped. He wanted to tell him, but he wasn't going to do it like this. When Jamie said those words to him, he wanted to be looking right into Chris's eyes. Wanted to see the love that Chris had given him unselfishly shining in answer, just for him.

Wanted to know inside that when he shared those words, gave them life and meaning, that there was no doubt. None about them, none about his wolf. That still gave him pause, but not as much as it had. He would face it without question that evening. It was the last battle he knew he really faced, and one he wouldn't regret or lose.

Nuzzling between shoulder blades to Chris's spine, he accepted that there was little that would change his feelings now. Not even facing a pack of wolves.

*I love you.* He tried it first in his thoughts. It felt right. And so did the man quivering beneath his weight.

Warm skin pulsed beneath his lips, light twitches that popped where he kissed. Flexes and little rolls that proved he was enjoying the close treatment and wanted more.

"Don't move," he breathed against Chris's neck. A murmur of assent solidified the strength of trust woven between them. He stepped away and rushed to grab what he needed. The last thing he wanted was to hurt Chris in any way.

He returned and immediately stripped out of his jeans. "Still okay?"

"Mmhmm."

*Sublime.*

With caring hands, he inched Chris backward. There weren't words to express how Chris affected him so Jamie showed him, nibbling and licking, teasing at but not giving relief where Chris wanted it most. Quiet moans floated through the kitchen, quick little gasps when the flick of a tongue or the nip of teeth found the most sensitive spots.

Jamie cupped the soft-skinned sac hanging between well-muscled thighs and watched in wonder as Chris's entire body trembled.

"So good."

Jamie couldn't believe this incredible man was lying still for him, allowing Jamie total control over his pleasure. He took his time showing him exactly how much he wanted Chris, how much this man had grown to mean to him. When he glided a slick-wet finger across his pucker Chris moaned, a deep, throaty sound that made the hair on Jamie's arms stand up. Electricity that seemed to amplify and grow with each touch and caress sparked between them.

He never stopped touching, never stopped moving as he drove Chris crazy. Chris's shoulders bunched and trembled as he gasped, his entire body vibrating with the growing need of his release.

"Jamie." It was a quiet whine.

"Want to make sure you're ready," he explained.

Chris pumped his hips. "I am!"

Jamie withdrew his fingers and quickly slid on the condom, taking a few slow breaths to prepare himself. He'd never been in this position, and hurting Chris was the absolute last thing he ever wanted to do.

Holding firm to strong hips he inched forward, his lungs lurching to a frozen halt when he breached Chris's heat for the first time. "Oh God." His focus, his world, narrowed to the sensations bombarding him.

"More," Chris choked. "Need…" The knuckles of his hands grew white as he gripped tighter, pushing into Jamie.

Jamie allowed his body to do things naturally, let his needs guide him. When he was fully seated he adjusted his feet, keeping Chris steady. Chris's hips jerked and he thrust, driving a grunt and gasp from Chris.

"Shit, yes," Chris said, moaning.

His muscles contracted, and Jamie saw white stars. Then he was moving, snapping his hips with sharp slaps of skin. The table bounced and skidded a little beneath the impact, but stayed steady.

Chris arched, pushing into each thrust in answer. Through slit eyelids Jamie saw his face tighten, his jaw lock down, and seconds later, felt the rocked shudder that hit him.

"Fuck! Yes!" Chris's shout filled the kitchen.

Jamie's heart slammed to a stop as he came, unable to withstand the heat, the scent, the feeling of Chris's climax.

He wobbled a little on knees that suddenly became water. Gasping, he bent over Chris's steady frame. Gusts of air rocked Chris's body. He wasn't moving any faster.

Leaning with his forehead to a shoulder, Jamie brushed light kisses to Chris's warmed skin. He could barely move. He couldn't think of any time he'd had that powerful of an orgasm.

Stretched out on the table against Chris's back, Jamie reached forward with a hand and clutched at one of Chris's, knitting their fingers together. He was all but on his toes, pressed into Chris's body. Neither seemed in a hurry to change that as the world stopped spinning for them.

## Chapter Twenty-Five

"Are you nervous?"

Jamie turned to see Chris in the dim cab of the truck. "A little. It's going to be a large group, and I only know about four of you." And once the pack was on the run, all four of those same men would be gone.

After their tryst in the kitchen and dinner, they'd showered and not long after that, Roman had called with the meeting place for the pack. Jamie knew they'd be gone for a few hours, so he'd brought one of his library books in case he didn't find any company to keep him awake. He wasn't exactly sure what to expect, if he'd be left alone because he was new, because he was there, or if the others would stay with him until the pack returned. He held his hands in his lap, the only sign of his insecurity.

Apparently, it wasn't missed by Chris. He reached over and covered his fisted hands. "It'll be okay. If it's like most nights, you'll either get your ear talked off by someone or find out everyone is just napping."

"I hope you're right."

A few minutes later, they turned onto an unlit dirt road that swerved and rolled like a river without a single straight line to it. After another twenty minutes, Chris pulled off onto a little-used rutted track that vanished within trees. When they emerged on the other side, Jamie spotted both Cade and Quade's vehicles, and at least a half-dozen more.

He hopped out of the truck and joined Chris by the bumper. Cade walked up first.

"How are you feeling?"

"Better. Back to work tomorrow."

Cade smiled. "Good to hear it. You've been missed." That warmed Jamie. He was wanted and needed, something that hadn't happened in a very long time.

Quade walked up to stand with Cade. He looked much more like his twin in shorts and a T-shirt.

"Let me introduce him around before we take off." Chris wound an arm around Jamie's waist.

"Sure. Tina and her mother should be here soon. I think they're all we're missing now."

"Tina?" Jamie never would have guessed.

Cade just shrugged. "You really can't tell unless you're one of us."

"How do you know?"

Chris tapped his nose. "Smell. There's a wild essence to a shifter that normal folks don't have."

"Wow," Jamie murmured.

He followed when Chris guided him around the group. Several warm and welcoming handshakes soon blurred, and he knew he'd never remember everyone's name the first time.

"When are you planning on doing the bonding ceremony?" one asked.

Chris cleared his throat, a hesitant catch in his answer. "Haven't talked about it yet."

Jamie gazed at him, sure the question on his tongue was clear in his eyes.

"When we get back, I'll explain," Chris offered. "Nothing big and scary, but it involves the pack when it's done."

"Oh." Jamie inched closer to Chris, not sure how to interpret that.

Another car arrived, and soon everyone was accounted for.

"Why not her dad?" Jamie whispered for Chris alone, gazing at a smiling and laughing Tina as she greeted everyone.

"He's probably working. He's one of Deputy Dave's boys."

"Oh. Really?"

"Yeah, we're a pretty tight town once you get into it."

"I'm beginning to see that."

"Come on. Time to go furry."

Jamie followed him back to the truck where Chris stripped without a blink of the eye to bare skin.

"Wait!" Jamie said before Chris could go any further. Chris's head snapped up from folding his shorts.

"Everything okay?"

"Just…" Jamie sidled in closer, body to body, uncaring that Chris was naked, more relishing that fact all over again. He wasn't sure why his heart was suddenly pounding like a hummingbird on the run, but he had to get closer to Chris. Had to feel his skin beneath his touch and know he was real. Just like this. Warm arms embraced him, and Jamie all but melted into Chris's chest. "I love you," Jamie said without reservation into the smooth skin of his neck. "No matter what, I'm here. I'm yours." He could face this; he knew he could accept Chris, on any terms.

The arms encircling him tightened into a vice. "I love you too, baby," Chris said, sounding more than a little choked up. He straightened to peer into Jamie's eyes. "Love you so much. So damned glad I found you."

Closing the gap between them, he kissed Jamie with enough heat and tenderness that Jamie was soon clinging more than leaning. And resenting the fact that Chris was naked when he wasn't, and that they wouldn't have time to do anything about either situation before he would be gone.

"I won't be long. I'll come back soon."

Jamie shook his head. "When you're ready. I'll be fine." He'd hole up in the truck and read.

Chris's gray eyes sparkled in the starlight. "You are amazing." He swept another kiss from Jamie. "Ready?"

"As much as I can be," Jamie replied, being wholly truthful. Who was ever ready to see a man become a wolf? Really?

Chris set him back on his feet, a small gap between them. Then, with mere inches between them, Chris's body shrunk, bending, with fur sprouting from skin.

"That is the most insane thing," Jamie muttered under his breath. Chris's dark wolf stood less than two feet in front of him. Cautiously, Jamie lowered to his knees on the ground. "I'll be here when you get back."

The wolf took a slow step forward, his head tilted.

"Yes, I promise."

Jamie swore the wolf smiled. He closed the gap and butted Jamie's chest with a hard head. Fur was warm and lush in his hand when he ran his fingers through it to stay steady.

"You are amazing," Jamie said in awe. The wolf raised his head to rub head to face. In that one motion, Jamie knew Chris was telling him how much he loved him.

Slowly, the other's sharp yips and barks infiltrated his thoughts as they gathered to run.

"Go." A quick grip on the wolf's neck ruff slowed his retreat. "Stay safe. Come back to me."

Another head butt was his answer. Jamie took it to mean he would do as Jamie asked. Then he twisted on his hind feet and loped to the center where about a dozen wolves had gathered.

Jamie watched in open-mouthed awe as the group jogged off into the night. Most were invisible, blending with the nighttime darkness in seconds, then they were all gone.

"They're quite the spectacle when you're new."

Jamie lurched to look over his shoulder. He planted a hand beneath him to get to his feet. "Barbara?"

"That's right." She smiled for him. "Tina likes it better when her father can run, but he can't always get running nights off with his schedule. And I don't let her come out here alone. She's safe, but she's still my daughter."

Jamie smiled. "I can understand that."

They chatted for a bit, helping Jamie pass the time. A few of the others who were left behind had disappeared into their vehicles, probably to sleep. Jamie didn't think there had been all that many that weren't gone with the pack.

"How long are they usually gone?" he asked.

Barbara moued her lips. "Depends, about two hours or so. Sometimes longer."

"That's not too bad," Jamie said.

"It's really not, and you get used to it."

Then something occurred to him. "You're not running."

She laughed lightly. "I'm not a shifter. I'm married to one." She leaned against the truck's side and crossed her arms. "Been with Lex almost twenty-five years now."

"Wow. Congratulations."

"He's a lug, and a bit of a pain being in law enforcement, but I love him to bits."

Jamie tried to think of who he had met since coming to town and couldn't place someone like her husband. "I haven't met him."

"He usually works nights, so I'm not surprised." They talked a bit more about the clinic, about the town, just small talk until she yawned. "Sorry."

"Why don't you go take a nap until they get back? I brought a book to read."

"Are you sure?"

He bumped her on the shoulder. "I'll be fine. Thanks for keeping me company to get used to this. They shouldn't be out too much longer anyway."

She looked at her wristwatch. "Probably not. Okay. You twisted my arm."

Jamie let her go without arguing. He needed a few minutes to think over what happened, with seeing Chris's wolf again, and close enough to actually touch him this time. It wasn't as shocking as the first time now that he knew what to expect, and just like he'd said, the wolf was more about snuggling than hurting him.

At least having someone to talk to for a while made it feel almost normal. Except for being out in the middle of nowhere after dark, surrounded by cars and a few people he didn't know. Except for waiting for his lover to come back from running as a wolf.

"Not exactly the kind of thing you can tell your best friend," he said under his breath, climbing into the cab of the truck. He stared out the glass in front of him, but little had changed. It was still dark and he was, for the most part, alone. Good thing his best friend happened to be the one who was currently out running as a wolf.

He dug the book light he'd brought out of a pocket and with his book in hand, tried to read.

* * * *

Chris loped into the gathering of cars and trotted over to the truck. It was dark inside, but a quick sniff proved Jamie was there. He let out a grateful breath and began the process of regaining his two-legged shape. At least it wasn't raining or worse. Being naked made bad weather miserable timing for runs. It wasn't uncommon to skip during the worst nights, but now he was more than thankful he'd been running the night they'd stumbled across

223

the one wanderer who'd changed everything about his world.

Opening the door he found Jamie stretched out on the seat, the book he'd been reading flat on his chest. He quickly slipped into his clothes, then tapped a calf on the sleeping hunk.

Jamie blinked with a startled gasp. "Oh, hi." He grinned in greeting and sat up, rubbing his eyes as he did.

"Let's go home."

Chris didn't argue when Jamie snuggled into Chris's shoulder, dozing again as Chris drove them home.

He hadn't run as long as some of the others, unable to stay away longer from Jamie. With an arm around his sleeping mate he almost hummed, even tired yet wired on the drive. Once they were home, he nudged a drowsy Jamie awake. "Come on, sweetheart. Let's go to bed."

"Mmmf," was the mumbled reply into Chris's shoulder, which made Chris chuckle. Making sure that Jamie could walk under his own power, he snatched the book and light off the console, shutting the truck door after them. It only took a few minutes to get them both inside and into the bedroom.

Jamie tried to help him undress, but Chris just pushed his hands away to do it for him. Half-asleep, he wasn't managing to do more than aimlessly shove things around. Once he was naked, he scooted Jamie closer to the bed. "Okay, baby. In you go. I'll be right there." Jamie rolled under the covers and curled up where he usually slept against Chris.

Chris quickly undressed and gathered their clothes to clean up, then joined him in bed. Jamie hardly moved other than to squeeze himself right up against Chris's side.

"Okay?" Chris asked, doubting he'd get an answer. He didn't. Tucking Jamie into his side and holding him close he fell asleep, so very thankful and living in the wonder of having Jamie's acceptance and love in his life.

## Chapter Twenty-Six

Jamie awoke with the brush of breath below his ear, moist and rapid. He'd awakened before the clock again, he thought as he became aware. The room was still in that gray-dark, dim-before-sunrise stage. Then he had the sensation that he was being watched and twisted his head.

A long pink tongue reached out and slurped his chin.

"Aahh!" He jumped from the bed in a rush to land on his feet with more of a wobble than he'd have liked. "Chris!"

He watched as the man in the bed regained his shape, having the balls to be laughing his ass off at Jamie at the same time.

He gripped a pillow and smacked Chris on the chest. "Ass!"

Chris only roared louder, clutching his middle.

"Not funny," Jamie fumed, glowering at the man in the bed.

"Come on," he said, gasping. He drew a couple breaths to ease his laughter. "I made him behave to let you sleep. He was curious, that's all."

Jamie threw the pillow at him, which Chris caught in a hand to stuff under his head. He opened up his arms. "Come here."

"I swear, you're schizophrenic." He climbed back into the bed. Though he went into the man's embrace, it wasn't exactly happily.

"And we love you," Chris whispered into his ear. "Couldn't live without you, baby."

Jamie went limp. Hard to stay mad at the jerk when he said stuff like that. A rush of the questions that had lumped up the night before hit him.

"How do you know what he wants?"

Chris settled them both more comfortably on the bed, taking a moment to answer. "It's like an innate desire, a want, I guess."

"So it's you, but not you?"

"Kind of. It's me, I'm still in there, but the wolf is a strong aspect. Like being so focused, so in tune to something, everything else fades away or goes to the outer perimeter of my consciousness."

"Wow," Jamie said breathily.

The shrill blare of the alarm clock made them both jump.

"Damn." Chris reached and smacked it. Hard.

Jamie grinned. "Come on, furball."

"Hey!"

This time when Jamie leaped from the bed, he was the one laughing. He dashed ahead of a swiped arm for the shower.

\* \* \* \*

Jamie opened the door on the truck and slid to his feet, waiting near the front for Chris to join him. They'd spent the afternoon looking at a couple cars and were now about to go have some downtime at the carnival in town for the July Fourth holiday.

Kids were squealing on one of the fast coaster ones that went forward, then backward. With the sun just starting to go down lights were beginning to sparkle, adding to the party atmosphere with the matching blared music. Jamie smiled at Chris when he palmed a hand to connect them.

"Anything you want to do?" Chris asked him.

Jamie hunted through the throng and finally shook his head. "Just walk around a bit, then maybe a few rides."

"Sure." Chris strolled easily with Jamie matching his pace, neither in a hurry to go anywhere or do anything. The Saturday patient run at the clinic had been lighter than usual, which gave them time to look at cars as Chris had promised. One pickup truck, an older Mustang, and two sedans. Not a bad selection, and they were within the range Jamie knew he could afford. He'd loved the Mustang, but knew he shouldn't get it just because it was a fast car.

"Hey, guys! Throw a dart!"

Jamie slowed and looked up. "A dart game?"

The guy behind the short counter didn't so much as blink at them holding hands. "Not just any dart game. Pop a balloon and win. Pop three and win big."

Chris snickered. "Does that work with the girls too?"

The guy laughed. "On their boyfriends. Every time." He winked and joked. "Give it a shot." He thrust three darts out.

"Okay." He shrugged, grinning at Jamie. "Guess it works on me too."

Jamie gave him a light shove, laughing at him. He glanced over the prizes and spotted a blue bulldog. "Get that for Mrs. Leal's daughter, Penny. Remember? She broke her arm riding her bike." They'd heard the story three times, in its entirety, when they brought in their German shepherd to be vaccinated.

"Good idea." Chris smacked a five on the wood. "Okay, line 'em up."

It took closer to fifteen than five, but Chris eventually got the dog. "Thanks," he said as he shook his head. "I was suckered."

Jamie wove an arm around his waist, giving him an appreciative squeeze. "Yeah, but she'll adore you for it."

Chris leaned over and kissed Jamie's temple. "You're sweet to think of it for her."

Jamie shrugged. "You're the one carrying around a blue bulldog now."

Chris held it out and snorted. Tucking it under an arm, he brought Jamie into his side with a matching looped arm and started walking again.

A group of kids, probably high school age, were just coming down off one of the rides, teacups or something that spun at a nauseating speed. One tugged a girl up close. Staring at them, Jamie froze in his tracks. Chris skipped a step, then stopped too.

"What's wrong?"

Jamie followed the group of kids with his eyes. Then the boy moved at a right angle. "That's him!" he whispered sharply.

"Him who?"

"The guy I chased when I fell into the washout ravine."

"You're sure?"

Jamie's heart was racing. "I'm positive."

"Okay. Hold Bluedog." Jamie scooped him out of Chris's hands and waited as Chris pulled out his phone and made a couple calls. "Keep an eye on him," he advised Jamie as they followed from a distance.

Jamie nodded. The brown hair, roughly six feet tall, lanky in a youthful way. He'd swear right to Deputy Dave's face that was the guy. He snatched a quick glimpse of a face and was just as positive now. Jamie watched as he walked through a gate to slip into another ride with his date, one that required padded braces and belts. Jamie's stomach plummeted. The kid had more balls than he did. He hated those rise-and-drop things.

"Okay. I've called the boys and the police. Just act calm and keep an eye on him without letting him know we are. They don't want us approaching him."

"It wouldn't be easy if we did. He's fast."

Jamie curled tighter against the stuffed bulldog. Anticipation made the moments drag even as the ride went quickly. They dismounted the ride and left the penned-off area. He knew it without a doubt now that he'd seen his face up front and closer. This was the guy—kid—he'd chased.

"Quit boring holes into him. He's going to catch on."

Jamie dropped his gaze, determined to not lose him through his lashes. They stayed behind the ticket stand, where they were hidden from view.

"Hey!" A hand fell on each of their shoulders.

They whirled in unison. "Ed!" Jamie's heart leaped. Talk about being snuck up on!

"Just seeing what you guys are up to," he said.

"Hanging out," Chris said, making a half-turn to swiftly gaze toward the ride. It was on its second rise to the top of the structure.

Jamie clutched at the dog which made Ed smile, albeit with a hint of longing. "Cute."

"It's not for me," he was quick to point out. "Mrs. Leal's little girl broke her arm last week."

"Uh-huh," Ed sassed with complete disbelief. "You two are almost too much, but you're still my friends, so…" He left it hanging.

"Asshole," Chris chimed with a kind grin. No hard feelings there.

"Yeah, yeah." Ed waved it off.

Jamie twitched to peek over a shoulder at the skyscraper ride. "He's gone!" The group of kids had vanished.

Chris whirled. "Shit!"

"Who?"

"He has to be here," Chris said. The two of them hopped around the stand they'd been hiding behind and aimed in the direction the kids had to have gone with Ed trailing, a little confused at it all.

"Who?" Ed asked again, now shadowing them.

"Jamie spotted the kid who started the fire at the clinic."

"Really?"

Jamie licked his lips, then nodded. "Yeah, and now I don't see him." He hunted through the scattered crowd, over heads and between bodies, as best as he could. Young girls ran for the merry-go-round holding hands.

Jamie edged to the side, stopping near a concession booth that was both crowded and busy, with the scents of cotton candy and hot dogs pouring from it. He looked and then looked again across the carnival grounds. He locked on the kid's eyes, which widened in recognition.

And just like before, he spun and launched in the other direction at a sprint. His date's wailing cry was lost in the sounds surrounding them and completely ignored.

"Shit!" Jamie tossed the dog at Ed. "Keep that!" Then he was hauling ass after the young man.

"Jamie!"

He didn't answer Chris's shout, slicing through the crowd, avoiding as many patrons as he could. He spotted the young man as he leaped a chain-link fence like it was a hurdle. Jamie lengthened his stride and paced himself, clearing the fence in a single launched stretch. His lungs burned as he breathed.

They raced, with Jamie gaining ground every second. Needing a nudge to catch his target, he rediscovered the anger this guy had caused by starting the fires at the clinic, by scaring Lyla with the fire in the Dumpster, for the damage to the storage shed.

His target tried to lose Jamie by jumping over things, another fence, and then a bike on a driveway, as they careened out into a street. Dogs barked as their feet slapped into pavement and soil. None of it slowed Jamie down one single step.

In the distance, over the pounding of blood and the gasp of air, he heard sirens and knew it wouldn't be long, but he couldn't lose him, either. Not now, not after he'd left Jamie unprotected and unconscious at the bottom of a ravine the first time.

Jamie growled and with mere feet between them, aimed for the guy's back and middle, taking him down with a hard shoulder tackle. They rolled, both grunting. Jamie was taken by surprise when the guy tried to pin him down.

He snarled and pushed back, toppling his attacker into the grass. With a quick twist and a roll, he had the guy face-first into the dirt with an arm bent backward and pinned over his spine under a sharp knee. He wasn't sure how he did it, but he managed enough and that was all that mattered.

"Don't move!" Jamie shouted from above him.

Beyond a shaken-up bounce and hard panting, he couldn't. "Come on," the kid whined.

"Shut up. I have nothing to say to you."

Desperate eyes tried to find him, then finally shut as he slackened into the ground. Jamie didn't take his focus away once when the car stopped at their side on the street.

"You can get off him now."

Cautiously Jamie did, obeying the sheriff, mincing a few steps away to give the officer room. A Jeep pulled up, and both Ed and Chris hopped out of it.

"Stand up slowly," the sheriff directed to the guy on the ground.

"Jamie!" He was engulfed in Chris's arms when he approached. Strength enveloped him as much as Chris's arms did. Chris dropped kisses, and Jamie soaked them up. "Are you okay?"

He nodded, still sucking air. "I'm fine. Tired," he managed. He sagged into Chris's strong chest and wrapped himself around him.

"Damn, Jamie. You can fly," Ed said with clear admiration.

"You're positive this is the guy, Jamie?" Chris asked.

The sheriff had him standing in handcuffs, but waited for a reply as well.

"It's him." He pressed his forehead into a strong shoulder, calming down as much as was possible.

"We'll run his prints against those found."

"I didn't do anything!" the guy screamed, jerking at the sheriff's hold, but he wasn't going anywhere other than where the sheriff put him. "He chased me! Arrest him for assault!"

They stood in silence as he was stuffed into the car, until the patrol car drove away. "Was he from Silo?" Jamie asked.

"I don't think so. Ed?"

"Don't recognize him. Maybe he's from Stiller Springs."

"Maybe," Chris allowed. He tipped up Jamie to get a good look at his face. "You're sure you're okay?"

Breathing more easily, he said, "Yeah, just a little tired."

Ed clapped him on the back, indicating a job well done. "Come on, hero. I'll buy you a drink at Mabel's."

Swallowing and feeling dry for the effort, Jamie thought that was the best idea of the night. "Thanks, Ed."

They all clambered into the Jeep and drove, at a more sedate pace than they had arrived, to Mabel's.

## Chapter Twenty-Seven

Jamie stirred. A pair of unblinking gray eyes were watching him from within a furry face.

"Chris," he mumbled. He buried himself into the soft pillow. "Why do you do that to me? Right when I wake up?" A pitched whine got Jamie to peek. He was then nuzzled and pushed against, prodded with a cold nose. Jamie lifted an arm and the wolf scooted closer, side to side with Jamie. "You're such a lover, aren't you?" A huff was the wolf's reply, but it made Jamie smile. He'd discovered Chris's wolf loved contact. It was like a pile of bodies, even if it was only the two of them. He'd even awakened with the wolf asleep, splayed across his chest. Jamie was Chris's, as he was the wolf's, and the wolf made no bones about showing that. Luckily, he really didn't do this all that often. Jamie was getting used to it, but right when he woke up... Yeah, that was just uncalled for. Waking with a wolf staring at you in the same bed was unnerving.

They'd received notification the day before from the sheriff's department that the guy Jamie had run down and tackled the night of the carnival had indeed been the one behind the hidden drugs and fires. After almost two months of investigation, he was finally permanently behind bars. Apparently, after a thorough search of his room at his parents', they'd found more evidence behind his drug concocting that tied him to the items and mess of the fire at the clinic that destroyed the shed.

They were all breathing easier knowing that the clinic was no longer under any kind of illegal shadow. The shed had been replaced several weeks before, and things were starting to return to normal.

Jamie had settled well into his place at the clinic. His dad was long gone, somewhere. He'd hardly given the man more than a thought since his unplanned arrival in Silo. Jamie even had his own car now. He'd bought the Mustang, though it wasn't unusual for Chris to drop him off and pick him up on their split days.

The sensation of skin and fur beneath his touch changed, breaking into his musings, and a moment later a naked Chris was in the wolf's place, curved around Jamie's frame beneath the sheets. He leaned forward and kissed Jamie's cheek. "Morning."

"Morning," he returned, offering a light peck on the lips. "Why this morning?"

"He likes you," Chris said simply. "Actually, he adores you. And sometimes he just wants to connect."

Jamie's lips edged northward. "I'll get used to it." He was already less disturbed than he had been the morning after he'd seen him run for the first time. They'd even played together out in the horse paddock once. That had to be progress, right?

Chris threaded his fingers into Jamie's hair. "You're handling it fine," Chris reassured him. He undulated closer, bringing their bodies length to length under the covers. A foot weaseled over a shin to land between his calves. Their warm skin grew hotter at the unassuming contact. "I can't help it, either," he said against Jamie's shoulder. "I always want to just touch you." He drew his tongue over Jamie's collarbone and moaned into his throat. "So he wants the same."

Jamie glided fingers across a flexing back and shoulders. He couldn't believe how his life had changed in the last few months. From homeless and practically on the run to having a job and living with an incredible man who loved him, that he loved, with a depth he'd never once expected to know. A gentle sigh slipped free when his lips continued to caress and drift over reawakening skin.

"I adore him too," Jamie whispered against Chris's ear. Chris's hold tightened in reply. Contentment ebbed through Jamie. There was no rush, no demand in their seduction. They didn't have anywhere to be this morning. It was decadent to hold, touch, and linger in their teasing and pleasing.

Chris's lips roamed, cutting tender wayward paths over Jamie's shoulders and chest, to weave upward to his neck. Jamie sighed, sinking into the ebbing warmth Chris created. The breath of words stroked his ear.

"Will you do the bonding ceremony with me?"

Jamie shifted to look toward his lover. "Is there blood, or knives, or anything like that?"

Chris chuckled roughly. "No. The reason it's hard for some is because it takes place with the whole pack."

Jamie brought Chris up by his chin to stare into his face to see him better. Soft gray eyes met his, full of all the love Chris gave him and more. "You mean that as *pack,* don't you? As in all furry?"

Jamie had been with the pack, but he had a feeling that this was a bit more involved and detailed than, say, just a midnight run.

"That's the hard part," Chris explained. "They're not going to hurt you, but the pack has to accept you as a new member, which also gives you everyone's protection."

"Protection?"

Chris nudged upward a little to be level with Jamie on the pillow. "As one of us you are just as important, and just as responsible, to keep our secrets safe."

Jamie gazed at him for a second. There was a wealth of meaning in those words. "Because you're hidden."

"Because we don't exist," he corrected evenly. He stroked a light thumb over Jamie's cheek. "To anyone outside."

"Did Ed know?" Jamie asked.

"No."

Jamie studied the face before him. What Chris was talking about went deeper than a marriage proposal. He would be responsible for Chris's life, not just his well-being. He would carry a secret that went beyond reality. He knew deep in his heart that he would guard that secret until the day he died.

Jamie took his time before saying anything, allowing the impact and the full weight of it to sink in. "I understand." He twisted to his hip to face Chris, reaching for his wandering hand. Cradling it in a palm, he kissed the center and closed Chris's fingers over it. "I absolutely want to."

Chris's lashes lowered for a heartbeat over an expectant gaze and he swallowed, a hard motion that Jamie could hear on the silence between them. "Love you so much, Jamie."

Jamie would never say as much, but he swore that Chris's eyes were moist. He inched as close as he could to Chris's front, touching in more places than not. "Love you right back…furball." Jamie knew that Chris spotted the twitch of his lips.

Chris groaned, then laughed roughly. "At least I'm *your* furball," he muttered as he rolled Jamie flat to his spine.

Gazing up into those gray eyes, feeling his heart begin to trip and his skin to burn, he happily agreed. "Mine. All mine." He sighed happily.

Then nothing else was said for quite some time.

## About the Author

Diana DeRicci is the sexy, flirty pen name of Diana Castilleja. A romance author at heart, DeRicci's writing takes you into a saucier spectrum of sensuality and sexual adventure, where a happily-ever-after is still the key to any story. Diana lives in central Texas with her husband, one son, and a feisty little Chihuahua named Rascal. You can catch the latest news on all of Diana DeRicci's writing and books on her website listed below. Feel free to drop Diana an e-mail. She'd love to hear from you.

Visit her online at:
www.DianaDeRicci.com

PURPLE SWORD PUBLICATIONS
Romantic Speculative Fiction
www.purplesword.com

www.ingramcontent.com/pod-product-compliance
Lightning Source LLC
Chambersburg PA
CBHW072221170626
46813CB00003B/1047